DARK THRESHOLDS

Exploring the Unknown, inspired by HP
Lovecraft & the Draconian Current

Webb, Page, Frønæs, Holmes,
Newman, Divinsky, Karlsson, Bert,
Hernandez, Schram, Kvarnbrink

Academia Draconis Publishing

Academia Draconis

ISBN-13: 9798523241291
ISBN-10: 1477123456

Cover art by: Ingvild Clark
Library of Congress Control Number: 2018675309
Printed in the United States of America

AUDIBLE CONTENT

Two aural transmissions of the Other

Free download and streaming at:
https://explorationsintotheunknown.bandcamp.com/

(The benefit from all voluntary purchases is donated to Dragon Rouge)

CONTENTS

EDITOR'S FOREWORD

Daring the Mysteries of the Mind

"Have you seen the gates of Deep Darkness?"

BOOK OF JOB 38:17

Max Ernst (1891-1976), who by many art historians has been dubbed the Quintessential Surrealist, put it this way: "Creativity is that marvelous capacity to grasp mutually distinct realities and draw a spark from their juxtaposition"

Grasping it seems, has fallen out of favor in this day and age of smartphones and search engines.
Where everyone has opinions but no one owns a dictionary anymore. Grasping and fumbling is not the same thing though people nowadays often get the two mixed up.

The grasping that Ernst is referring to entails a courage few possess. It means inviting alien influences, it means owning up to the shortcomings of knowledge, it means letting go of safety, it means daring to tread that familiar path everybody stumbled across in childhood but most have conveniently forgotten.
-Where there are no guides save our own shaky convictions. It's not just the road less traveled. It is a road that is, in the ultimate sense, always traveled alone.

-A road where we for good or ill end up meeting our deepest selves and in this sense, it has much in common with the initiatory spirit journeys described in Shamanic cultures.

Therefore, one would do right to be scared as it might just as well lead to madness and ruin instead of triumph.

In the Great Unknown, no excuses are acceptable and all consequences are absolute.

HP Lovecraft may to have been more aware of this than most and even if biographers have often portrayed him as a shy and neurotic recluse, he clearly lived his inner life on cosmological frontiers lightyears away from 98% of the humanity of his day.

For dear readers, contrary to what the institutions of the world would have you believe; it has always "been within the mind of Man to draw the Grand Design".[1] -To soar if you will, on the winds of "pure Mathematics" where any problem by necessity has a solution provided the enquirer can muster the fortitude to formulate the equation correctly within.

What happens to you when the design is completed or the equation balanced? Well, that must each intrepid explorer discover for him or herself.

-Bon Voyage!

Jens Frønæs

Stavanger, Norway. Midsummers Eve 2021

INTRODUCTION

The Apocryphon of Howard P

By Thomas Karlsson PhD

"Το Απόκρυφον Νεκρονομικόν!" Necronomicon Apocryphum. A creeping feeling of discomfort came over me. Not as something malicious but as something disharmonious. Much like the rushing reverberation caused by a dentist drilling into your teeth though on an abstract, incorporeal level. In addition, I heard a cutting sound. It sounded like a squeaky door or as if someone was sawing through metal. I took a few deep breaths and focused my attention on the sigil in front of me. It came from a manuscript I had received from a small exclusive occult society that had just handed me a large bundle of documents.

This material included writings from occultists such as Kenneth Grant and Michael Bertiaux, copies from Black Books and Grimoires such as Le Dragon Rouge, Grimorium Verum and Petit Albert as well as a lot of writings I even today haven't been able to pinpoint the origin of. The document in which had found the sigil I had a Greek title but had evidently been translated into English second hand. Its paper was old and cheap and had been clumsily stapled together. Its letters punched in ink from an old-fashioned typewriter.

"Το Απόκρυφον Νεκρονομικόν!", the apocryphal Necronomcion. There are a number of biblical texts not recognized by the Church that came to be known to posterity as the apocryphal writings, including the Gospel of Thomas, the Gospel of Judas, and the Gospel of Mary Magdalene. The Necronomicon proper is a mysterious book alluded to in the stories by H.P. Lovecraft and there have been a quite few published works claiming to be genuine article, which according to Lovecraft was originally called Al Azif and written by the "mad Arab" Abdul Alhazred. Occultists like Kenneth Grant have argued that the true Necronomicon does exist as a kind of astral book, even if it was invented by Lovecraft. Several occultists have argued that Lovecraft channeled knowledge from the dark dimensions of the Universe and that the contents of his books are more than fiction.

One of his strongest quotes comes from the introduction to his famous short story The Call of Cthulhu; "We live on a placid island of ignorance in the midst of black seas of infinity, and it was not meant that we should voyage far. " Lovecraft's worlds constitute a kind of reverse Platonism, where we ought to live happily unaware of the stark truths that brood just beyond our perceptual limits. While Plato taught that one reaches enlightenment through the Good, the True and the Beautiful, the protagonists in Lovecraft's short stories usually end up panicked and bat shit crazy after glimpsing the wonderful realities that are out there. Somehow both are right. Reality beyond the human consensus-bandwidth is terrifying because it overturns our whole way of understanding life. In myths from all continent's dragons, monstrous beasts and demons lurk at the threshold of our world ready to pounce on us without warning.

From a Draconian perspective though, these entities are only terrifying before we get to know them and begin to learn about dimensions beyond our own. In this way we become more "demonic" ourselves, by learning to see and hear in the same way as the demonic powers that hide in the unknown, in dark matter, dark energy and in solar systems that are appreciated by black holes.

The sigil in front of me glowed with a cool green tone. It was placed upside-down behind a crystal ball, so that looking through its round surface the sigil was reflected right side up. What the right direction is supposed to be can in itself be difficult to ascertain with occult sigils. In addition, the perspective starts twisting, developing into 3D and a number of things start to happen. Not infrequently it starts to move and the image comes to life. That is why it is such a powerful method of working with sigils. Neither in the George Hays' Necronomicon nor in the much more famous "Simonomicon" had I found a sigil resembling the one I was working with, but there was one of somewhat similar design in Johannes Faust's "Magia Naturalis et Innaturalis", a German Black Book from 1849.

"Το Απόκρυφον Νεκρονομικόν!" Johannes Faust's Magia notwithstanding, in all probability there have never been a Necronomicon before Lovecraft, but even the majority of well-known Grimoires and books on the dark arts are filled with fictitious claims, a fact that doesn't make them any less powerful as magical items or valuable as artifacts of cultural history. In this respect Grant`s idea of a kind of Astral Necronomicon feels entirely possible. A great work of art does not diminish in its greatness if either its creator nor its paramour's, generations after the artists death, creates myths around it. The work itself carries qualities beyond time and space. Kenneth Grant's books should be taken with many pinches of salt, but they function as surrealistic works of art with great magical potential. The risk with works with an overly frivolous view of sources and less than stable anchoring in reality is that they become pure fantasy products that only reflect the author's own personal microcosm.

Dr. Stephen E. Flowers has combined academic rigor with magical practicality to an exemplary degree. In many ways, Flowers and Grant are polar opposites of modern Left Hand Path occultism but both have indisputable qualities as occult authors in a subculture that is otherwise largely characterized by superficiality and sensationalism disseminated through incoherent and poorly arranged books.

The sigil, whatever its physical origin, emitted a strong force that quickly bound me to powers outside our ordinary cosmos. The entire room began to glow in the cool green color that now surrounded the sigil. Moving inside the crystal ball it seemed to take on an intricate 2-dimensional shape. At the same time the room filled with whispers that cut through marrow and bone. The sigil began to crawl out of the crystal ball and into the room by the way of fast-growing tendril-like "roots". Then suddenly, through the crystal balls reflection, I saw a figure standing behind me. It resembled a man in a black cloak. It too was entirely made of a network of shadowy roots. It gave off a putrid odor of decay. My instinct made me want to turn around, but I knew that that would probably cancel the experience, so I continued to focus on the crystal ball. "Welcome" I whispered. The creature did not move but gave off another foul odor. I tried again to communicate with it, but each time it gave off more and more strange odors. Some disgusting, others rather pleasing. It struck me that it might be trying to communicate with scents. I reached for a number of plant essences and tried to formulate a message by mixing them intuitively. Lo and behold, we achieved communication through scents! It "said" it came from one of the tunnels between the A'arab Zaraq Qlipha and the Gamaliel Qlipha. The true number of tunnels is significantly more than the 22 or 24 with which we normally structure occult reality according to modern Kabbalistic models. These models of spheres and tunnels give us adequate maps but a map that is not the same as the actual terrain. There was something beautiful and melancholic but at the same time threatening about the creature. It was not a demonic intelligence but something else. It communicated with me and declared that it had "died a hundred deaths" and got lost in the qliphotic tunnels.

It asked for my help. "I need your fire to find out of the darkness," it suffused, then violently tried to grab hold of my inner fire, my Prana. I was close to fainting and had shortness of breath. I started mumbling the barbarous words from the Dragon Ceremony.

"Lepaca Kliffot!" The strangulation of my inner fire hardened and I had to fight not to lose consciousness. "Marag Tehom!" The creature radiated desperate aggression and roots began coiling around my feet. When I came to the last and decisive words of power: "Ho Drakon Ho Megas!" the creature began to burn. The Great Dragon had sent a beam of fire towards it incinerating it completely in a matter of seconds while it farted its last heart wrenching scream! It was gone and the room was restored to some manner of normality. Behind the crystal ball, the sigil had fallen over.

PUMPKINS

by Don Webb

Phillip Brasingame was my customer for many months before he became my tenant. He was a good customer. He was a good tenant. I think he was a good man, perhaps with just too active an imagination. I don't think he meant for it to happen. No, I don't think that at all.

I may have been the real world friend that new him best. I know he had online friends that were very serious mathematicians with lots of letters after their name, and he had lots of Facebook occultist friends with names like "Thee Demon Azathoth." The press made a big noise about the latter and most of them seemed to vanish like cockroaches encountering the light. The former was a bit too obscure for them to think about. Of course I got mentioned in two articles in the *Austin American Statesman* and Libby's Books got mentioned once. Of course that was at the first part, at the second part—the more plainly horrific part—he wasn't mentioned, but that was my fault not his.

Libby's Books was in the wrong section of town for a bookstore. It was at the end of a strip mall in the St. John's neighborhood, which is the likeliest place to meet a crackhead. It had been a bookstore for 35 years. The neighborhood around had rotted. I lived in that neighborhood, on a semi-undecayed block. I had moved into my Mom's house the year of my divorce to take care of her. She died three years later. I didn't feel much like being a technical writer then and one day, buying vintage SciFi at Libby's, I asked if he needed an assistant. Nowadays Libby is in a home and the shop is just me. The rent is low and Libby's secret porn room has enough older male customers to keep the lights turned on. The general room has its regulars—romance, westerns, SF, and the like. About half my customers are white. It is a premier store for "Blerds"—their term—black nerds. There were three main customers: Malcolm Briscoe, Abdullah Loggins, LeRoy Green. LeRoy later got a lovely glasses-wearing young woman, LaTonia Washington. I met Phillip there. He was in his mid-twenties, unlike the teenaged blerds, but he was pointing out Samuel Delaney's shorter novels to the blerd tribe. When he came to the counter, I complimented his taste. He was carrying a stack of mathematics magazines—Libby would buy anything—but technical journals on higher maths aren't a big seller. I think they had lain there for seven years. He also had a rather shady occult book, the **Codex Catamaco,** a "Mayan grimoire" that had briefly been popular in 2012. He looked a little embarrassed, I assume by the occult book. Hell, I sell stained copes of *Nuns in Bondage,* who am I to judge.

He became a regular after that. He bought all of the math from the store, all the weird fantasy—Lovecraft, Smith, Kline—even crap like *Lucifer's Aces.* He was a student at University of Texas going for a PhD in "hyperbolic geometry". Go ahead Google it, I did. He drove a shitty car, dressed from Goodwill, and had taped glasses. One day he said he was about to be thrown out from his apartment near campus. I told him I had a room over my garage that I rent cheaply. It was a done deal. He would pony up seventy-five in cash every week and it was just between us.

I liked the pen money and I liked having someone nearby. My friends had largely left the city over the last decade after the tech bubble burst. Phillip tolerated my stinky old tomcat. He came over for chili on Saturday nights and we watched *Dr. Who.* Naturally we talked about time, space, and other dimensions. He was a believer, well I guess that's the wrong word, he had a good scientific understanding of M-theory and some unusual notions of access to other dimensions.

"There's more around us than we can see, but perhaps some of it we can interact with. Maybe that's the mechanism of synchronicity. Maybe that causes 'serialism.' The phenomena of an unlikely event repeating itself again in a single life."

I like this sort of speculation. It made my ex-wife crazy. So I say, "I've always thought that higher dimension stuff was mental. If I can conceive of a four-dimensional solid, I must have a five-dimensional mind."

Phillip looked at me like I was simple-minded and we stopped that line of discussion. He moved in March, and the week before Halloween he confessed his dark secret. I don't drink, except in October—I'm crazy for pumpkin beer—so I'd bought a six pack of pumpkin ale and Phillip, knowing my weakness for pumpkin beer, bought a six pack of pumpkin beer. After *Dr. Who* and *The Navy versus the Night Monsters,* I realized he had had ten beers. His story was very boozy, but I think I got most of it.

His mom had been in some cult in Los Angeles in the '80s. When he was a kid they either had more money than they could jump over, or be literally living out of their car. The cult wanted something from her, some sacrifice, possibly Phillip. She did a ritual and called up the cult's god, "a polychromatic hypersphere", and offered herself in exchange. Phillip saw a mass of glowing globes surround her and pull her off screaming into another dimension (or as he tried to explain to me, unobservable parts of this dimension). But he knew It would find him some day, tracking on the spirals of his DNA. He broke into drunken tears a couple of times while he was explaining the science of this. He likened human flesh to old style punch cards (for the IBMs I grew up with). He said these multidimensional beings were like vast computers that needed living beings for input. I couldn't follow his explanation but he was sure it was based on the structure of DNA. He had come up with a comic book solution. He would contact the hypersphere and make a deal with it. Sorcerers had done so aeons ago, and if he could visualize the right model of the creature/god/hypercomputer/Old One, he could talk to it.

I let him sleep on the old convertible sofa in the living room. Of course I didn't believe in monsters from dimension X, but I could believe that the right cultic environment aided by LSD, PCP —and the stress of economic woes in Hollyweird—would let a little boy see his mom's death as an extraterrestrial fantasy. When he woke up, he was embarrassed. He told me a hundred times that he had just been drunk, that he was sharing a plot for a science fiction story. He was a terrible liar but I could tell it was important to him that I believed it. So I never mentioned it again.

Sometimes very late at night—four, four-thirty—I could hear chants, see strange lights from his room. Well, he didn't seem to be building fires.

Months went by. Christmas brought a little more business to the shop and around Valentine's, Phillip showed up grinning from ear-to-ear.

"I just had a long chat with Aunt Jane. I am adopted! Mom had been briefly married in LA and they had adopted me, then dad ran off. I have no DNA ties to her."

The chanting stopped. The weird strobe lights at predawn stopped. He dressed better. He dated. He was elected to some office in the graduate students' association.

Then came April. He sold most of his occult books to the store, as well as a ton of the weird fantasy stuff. I even ran an ad in Craigslist for a couple of days and got some real odd folk to drop by and drop cash. It was a beautiful Austin spring. Bluebonnets filled the roadways, little rainstorms at night. Phillip won a prize at the University of Texas Math department for "groundbreaking work in four-dimensional topology, symplectic geometry and gauge theory, and for his remarkable use of ideas from physics to advance pure mathematics." Which means Phillip really was much, much smarter than me.

On the 30th a hell of a thunderstorm came. I usually kept the shop open to six—nine on Thursdays—but listening to the storm-tracker, I decided to close by four. No sane person would risk hail and/or tornado to buy old paperbacks. Even the pervert crowd has limits. I walked home. It was windy as hell and began to rain just as I turned onto my block. The drops fell fat and cold and with speed. I saw the lights were on at Phillip's. I went up the shaky steps and pounded on his door.

"Are you OK?" I asked.

"Sure," he said. "It's just a storm. UT closed at noon though, the officials are worried about flood."

"You want to come down for chow?"

He thought about it.

"Nah. I've got a little pot of soup going. And thirty pages of a paper due."

"If there's a tornado, you should come down; we'll sit in the bathroom and play chess. There's no windows there."

"Thanks. You guys take weather more seriously than we do."

I ran downstairs, both soaked and cold, I turned the TV on to the Weather Station, and lost myself in a Robert Silverberg paperback from the '70s. The rain really picked up and the gales shook the stucco-covered walls of my little house. The lights flickered, and the storm cell filled up most of the radar screen. I thought about ordering a pizza then decided that would be too tough on the delivery guy. The wind didn't seem to be letting up. A small tornado was spotted in Doublesign about forty miles south of me. Small hail started to fall. Few cars were on the street. A few blocks away on Cameron I heard an ambulance and a fire truck. I made a sandwich of turkey pastrami and American cheese and read some more. The storm began dying down about eight. By ten it was done; the clouds parted and a very silvery full moon made the rain-glazed world sparkle. I watched the local news, they said another cell was due after three. It would be the "bad one." I unlocked my backdoor in case Phillip needed shelter. I cracked the windows slightly, crawled under my burnt orange comforter, and went to sleep.

The dream was peculiarly vivid.

I was walking in the park next to my childhood home. Sam Houston Park had a football field in the middle, swings on one side, and was ringed with Chinese elms. It was a pretty spring day; there were some kids on the swings, opposite my side of the park. The park sloped gently where I entered from the southeast corner. At the northwest base was a small outdoor theater. I saw a clown selling balloons. Everything was exaggerated as it often is in a dream. He had a huge mass of balloons of every color. His harlequin costume had diamonds of every shade. He was tall and thin and looked like Ronald MacDonald, or maybe Pennywise from Stephen King's *It.* I knew it was a dream and upbraided myself for such a schlocky image. I walked across the football field and approached the clown. He smiled with his bright red mouth. I could hear calliope music from somewhere, annoying flute-like whistles. Knowing this was a dream I walked up to him.

"Hello Donald." He said.

I've always hated *Donald.* I'm Don, just Don.

"Do you want to buy a balloon?"

"Yes, I want all of your balloons."

"Well, my balloons might want you. You can hold them for now."

He handed me all of the balloons. All of their strings were woven into a rope. As I took them, the rope became a semi-transparent, sticky cord. It wrapped around my little fist like five times, and then the balloons began to tug me upward. I tried to let go. I grabbed at the rope with my other hand, and my other hand stuck to the cord as well. I kicked and tried to force myself down. I was rising swiftly. I was already thirty feet in the air. I was screaming for my dad. The suspension hurt my arms; I felt them tearing out at the socket. Some people say you can't feel pain in dreams. Some people are wrong. The kids at the swings ran over to watch. The clown was petting a little girl's black hair while looking up at me, laughing. The balloons were rising faster now. I was a hundred, maybe two hundred feet in the air. I saw where they were taking me. A massive cloud of spheres rolling against each other. Pulsing, living, vast. Perhaps a mile across. Between the spheres was thick, red oil. Some of it was falling on my face and exposed arms. It burned, like dry ice burns. I stopped remembering this was a dream. I could remember something on the radio about a UFO. I screamed and screamed.

And woke myself up. The wind was pounding my house and the rain/sleet mix was overpoweringly loud. I looked at my alarm. Four-thirty. I got up and lightning flashed, followed by a deafening roar. The bolt must have been in my yard. I was deafened and also confused, because when my eyesight came back the power had gone off. My old tomcat Shem was howling at the top of his lungs. There was a rumbling outside. Tornado? I couldn't find my smartphone in the dark. I kept a candle in my nightstand with a box of matches. I've had to use it exactly twice in 20 years, but it was where Mom kept it. It was one of her rules—like always have a can of soup in your house in case you get sick and don't want to go shopping. I lit the candle. Lighting flashed again four times in a row. One of the blasts seemed to be green, the last one purple. I ran to my backdoor. There was light in Phillip's apartment. How could that be? My lights were out. It was a weird, multicolored light. Then I could hear his screams; the storm noises were louder. I paused to pull on pants and ran out into the night. I nearly fell twice as I went up the rain-soaked stairs. At the top, the door was locked. I pounded. I couldn't hear Phillip anymore, just a loud white noise hiss as if all the transistor radios in the world had decided to howl at once. I fumbled the keys out of my pants pocket and put them in the lock.

I hate to admit this, but I hesitated at that moment. The nightmare still clung to me like a wet T-shirt and the beery confession of six months ago seemed very plausible. Then I regained myself. This was my home, my land, and had been my mother's home. I threw open the door.

Half the room was filled with glowing spheres rolling against each other over Phillip's twin bed. I couldn't see him. Their hiss filled my ears and my mind. They were shrinking. Lightning struck the mass—or shot out from the mass through the roof. This knocked me down the stairs. It took a few minutes to get back on my feet and back into the apartment. There was a jagged hole through the roof; the mattress on the bed had caught fire and the fire had been extinguished by the rain. The room stank like burned hair, cat litter, and bus exhaust. I could barely hear anything, but over the ringing in my ears I made out the sound of a fire truck. Suddenly there were strange lights in my front yard. Red and blue.

It was the fire truck a neighbor called. The firemen were rushing by, down the stairs. I couldn't understand them, but I made them understand that I was the landlord looking for my renter. They had huge flashlights and searched Phillip's flat. They found nothing, but there were strange, burnt organic masses on the bed. He could've been vaporized. Over my protests they took me to the hospital. I tried calling Phillip and left a message. It turned out his phone was sitting on the dresser, quite unharmed.

It was a great story for the paper. "Local Man Vaporized by Lightning". I threw away the stinking mattress and my insurance paid for fixing the roof. Otherwise, there was strikingly little damage. I got a nasty letter from the city about renting without a permit, but in light of the disaster they declined to press charges. I was interviewed by the local paper. And it was forgotten.

I had real problems sleeping after that. My doctor tried three levels of sleeping pills—it pretty much took industrial strength. To my surprise I had no nightmares, at least nothing beyond the going-to-school naked sort of thing. After the roof was fixed, I kept the apartment locked up. My neighbors were nice; they brought me a few casseroles and even walked over to my shop and forced themselves to buy something.

In the summer Libby died and left the store to me. I figured his son would protest the move, but he lived in Florida and didn't care. He didn't even go to the funeral. Over the next few months I visited Phillip's Facebook page and sent messages to all 111 of his friends that he had died of lightning, and gave a link to the article in the *Austin American-Statesman* article. Some of his occultist friends made dire remarks about his passing on Walpurgisnacht. Some of his math friends thanked me. Once nice girl even said she was sorry for my loss. I called UT of course. I was hoping to track down his Aunt Jane. After all he had left behind a computer, a dresser full of poor grad student clothes, and some books. I never found her. In August, Shem wandered over to Cameron road and spent the ninth of his nine lives. It took me a couple days to find the body. I scraped it off the road and buried it in my back yard.

When October rolled around I drank my pumpkin beer

every night and felt sorry for myself. I was sad because I could tell no one. I had my own theories of course. I think his years of trying to visualize the hypersphere had caught Its attention. It came at a time when the world is open—April 30 and Halloween are the traditional times. I thought about writing to paranormal researcher but I didn't want the questions. I was 60 and, for the first time in my life, I began to feel tired. I decided to sell Phillip's books. I had no right to do this of course, but I wanted closure. I gave his clothes and his computer to Goodwill.

The blerds bought them all. They wanted to do something in memory of his passing. LaTonia pointed out that with all the horror Phillip liked to read, a big Halloween bash might be the best memorial. They could show movies at the Community Center and decorate the neighborhood. Only after they left the store did I realize they took the two spiral notebooks that Phillip kept with his books. I had glanced through them once. They were full of very precise drawings of spheres, cubes, tesseracts, and hyperspheres, as well as mathematical formulae with several references to John Milnor's seven dimensional manifolds. I tried Googling that and just felt dumb, although I did learn a term from differential topology, "exotic sphere." Oh well, I thought, those kids are a lot smarter then me, maybe they could find meaning there. Maybe they could bring a positive spin on everything.

The kids put out fliers promising a haunted house and a party. They bought all the pumpkins from St. Mark's Methodist Church pumpkin patch. They painted some of them, made strange jack o'lanterns of others. They exhausted the Party Pig's supply of faux spider web and draped it everywhere in the six-block radius. They put up fake tombstones and big statues of "elder gods." They encouraged folks to decorate their yards and they put up posters with Phillip's pictures everywhere. They even bought candy for low-income households to give out, and helped kids get costumes.

They invited everyone in a six-block radius to the event. They pestered me every day until I said I would go. On Halloween night, the moon was cantaloupe full and as lovely as the night Phillip was taken away. The party was being held in the community center about three blocks from my home. My street was alive with trick-or-treaters. I walked down to the community center. In twenty years in this neighborhood, I had never seen as much Halloween activity. Cars drove slowly down the streets, young couples walked arm-in-arm.

The pumpkins were everywhere. The kids must have bought hundreds of them but they weren't right somehow. They were oddly spaced. Some in clusters, some singly. Some of them had been died green, red, or purple. They didn't have faces. They had mathematical symbols carved in them, illuminated from within by small white candles. Some of the symbols were complex and looked more like the seals of demons from magic books.

These were the spheres from Phillip's notebooks. The trick-or-treaters, my neighbors, and I were inside a model of the hyper-sphere that had carried Phillip away. Just as I turned to run, the jack o'lanterns began to roll toward me. A couple rose into the air. One flew into me. I could smell the pumpkin guts, and the wax from the candle splashed on my face, near my eyes. I could hear screaming. I tried to keep running and then there were more of them. One flew between my legs and spread me open and lifted me off the ground. They all spun and I was put together with small children, and then dogs and cats. And we all screaming, howling. Lights began flashing over the surface of the pumpkins —white, green, red, purple, and orange. They pressed harder and blood began to act as a lubricant. I could feel they were dragging us upward and away—away from the world of four dimensions and five senses. My nose was broken and I saw bits of children's mask in the spinning red goo.

We were being made into the hypersphere god. We were being broken up and reassembled. I was coming into contact with Phillip's mind (well parts of it), and his mom, and a thousand human and pre-human sorcerers that had called to this Old One. My limbs were torn off, and my memories, and that rather vague thing I had called a soul. The assimilation was painful in ways humans have never know pain. And it...

It

It

It took much, much longer to do so than we could have imagined in our worst nightmares.

INITIATION

By Judith Page

The seeker of mysteries stood inside the passage, letting her eyes grow accustomed to the dark. Cautiously she inched her way along a massively thick wall. At times, she thought she heard a drumbeat, but it was her heart pounding in her ears. Down and down she crept, passing crypts and caverns. Each turn she made led to more confusing winding tunnels.

If only someone could guide me through this puzzle, she wished.

Deeper into the bowels of the labyrinth she wandered. The little beetle that had attached itself to her robe scuttled off into the darkness. Suddenly a voice boomed at her like thunder.

"Hasten back to your city, back to all who are faint-hearted," it screamed.

"I won't listen to you. You don't scare me," she returned in defiance.

The voice continued to mock her with cackling laughter.

"I don't need anyone's help. I'll be my own guide in this darkness, and I'll leave with the golden ankh of courage," she retaliated.

Slowly, the seeker moved through the blackness, aware of the many phantoms. She felt their soft hands pulling at her robe and heard their whispers that echoed through the hallways. They spoke the language of the old ones from the first time. The history of the labyrinth began to unfold.

A familiar voice whispered to her in the darkness. "I give you a riddle, Seeker: Life is white, and death is dark; life and death are drawn in circles, ever-diminishing concentric circles, a confusing mass of blind alleys that mirror images back and forth." It hissed and she saw the glow from its scaly body as it slithered ever nearer to her. "If you care to follow me, I'll tell you all you desire. I'll show you wonderful things, earthling, as only I know the secret of immortal life. Come, come with me, Seeker. I'll reward you by giving you the golden ankh of courage."

I'm so tempted—anything to find the ankh and just get out of here, she thought. She recalled the words of her master: "Take care. Do not believe all that is said to you."

"You're lying. I don't believe you have this ankh."

Its body slithered around her and gave off a sickly smell of musk. Suddenly, the scaly form towered over her, spitting venom in her face. She fell back in fright and raised the hand wearing the ring of magic.

Without warning the ground sagged like a sky cloud under the girl's weight. All became strange as the earth bent, making crackling noises beneath her feet. Like clouds being swept away from heaven, she tumbled about on a dizzy, swimming earthscape, losing all sense of direction.

An invisible force pushed her down through a narrow passage, where she could no more feel wandering spirits or hear their inner ravings. She heard only the drum of silence. Through this silence, she heard the magic and listened to the secrets.

"To solve this ancient puzzle is to solve the puzzle of the labyrinth," a voice said. "Walk anti-clockwise and unwind all that you know."

This confused her. Which way should she turn?

Invisible hands touched her shoulders from behind and swung her round to the left.

More passageways presented themselves, most of them leading to an abrupt end. For an eternity, she wandered, feeling her way through the maze. As she touched the surface, it gave enough light to reveal carvings of the forty-two demons. She quickly jerked her hand away, for fear of awakening them to her presence. Too late!

"We know you're here," they groaned in unison. The wall poured out creatures with heads of snakes, vultures, hawks, and rams. Each one held a knife. They barred the only doorway. She was surrounded, with no way to escape.

Suddenly an invisible force field emerged, giving the seeker enough time to make a dash for the doorway. Pitch-blackness greeted her. She stumbled, groping her way along another wall.

"Light my way," she commanded, turning the ring on her finger. The stone floor beneath her feet glowed a phosphorescent green, lighting the way towards the middle of a large chamber.

Exhaustion overtook her. Very sleepy, she lay down on her bed of silence in the centre of the labyrinth on an island surrounded by black flames that burned with the flame of eternity.

Around her, the air split in two, as the great lord, Sobek, appeared. His reptilian head on the body of a man. Proud and regal, the god stood, holding the Uas sceptre in Set's likeness. He looked upon the sleeping girl, and in her dream state, he spoke to her: 'Ask of me all you search for, but speak in riddles; speak in my tongue, lest all others hear your questions.'

The seeker uttered soul sounds in the ancient tongue of Sobek. Pictures flashed before her, each appearing in a separate chamber, and each one had its own meaning.

Thousands of lines were written. She learned the ways of medicine, read the secrets of charms and magic and how to use them. She relearned the magic of her name and the mystery of its sound. Her name became her password that bridged earth, sky, and heaven.

With a touch as light as a feather passing across her face, Sobek spoke in a voice that echoed throughout the centre of his labyrinth, out into the passageways, and into all the rooms and beyond for all to hear: "From henceforth, you will be known as Meri-Khem. With my blessing, take the ankh of courage with you."

From the land of sleep and silence, Meri awoke, clutching the golden ankh of courage. Clockwise, she retraced her footsteps. Along winding pathways and darkened corridors that housed shadowy forms, she walked, tall and proud.

This time, she heard whispers of a different kind. They were the lost souls crying from their darkness. All were fated to wander in the maze of the labyrinth forever. Were these the seekers who didn't make the journey?

Each one now pleaded, "Take me with you. Take me with you."

No, Meri knew these were her discarded thoughts and worn out memories of a previous life, of a death and rebirth. Onwards and upwards she went, out of chaos and confusion and into a world of harmony and order, of mind and emotions.

She stood taller in the sunshine near the shadow of the Mastaba that housed the fearful labyrinth.

"It was a great testing for you in the inner sanctum of the heartland of Sobek, priestess," the master said, bowing low: "Your mind is a labyrinth, likened to a many-roomed palace. Many seekers have faced their limits and have visited only just a few rooms, leaving the rest in total darkness. And in those rooms they chose to visit, only a few windows were ever opened. This is likened to the darkness and ignorance of the mind." He drew in his breath, and continued, "You have been to all these rooms in your mind and in the maze and have awakened your senses to question everything. You see, Meri-Khem, the only evil that exists is the evil of ignorance."

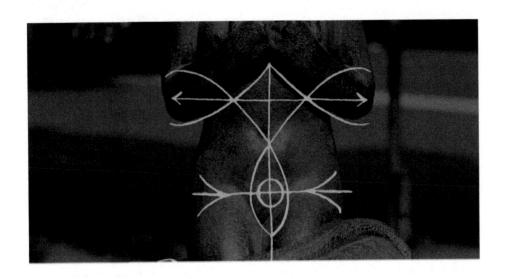

SATARIEL'S CHOSEN

by Jens Frønæs

«Our mythology now is to be of infinite Space!»

-FROM «MYTHS TO LIVE BY» BY JOSEPH CAMPBELL

The rain kept pouring down and the Oslo summer skyline had gained an unsavoury shade of pale orange, like spoiled drying meat inside a leftover mussel, when Professor Johan Ystad finally decided to get to his appointment. Most of his colleagues at the faculty of Religious History were long gone on some much-needed vacation or at least at home with their families. Ystad had no children, no wife either so he didn't mind being asked to cover for them on a regular basis. Actually, it suited him well, as he had long since realised that he didn't like being at home all that much. The stark solitude of that place was just too much of a reminder of a certain choice he had committed pretty early on in life.

He made a quick scan of his office. To his right were the windows overlooking the main courtyard at Blindern. To the left were his overburdened bookshelves that also housed the speakers of his modestly equipped but pricey Bang & Olufsen Stereo system. Right in front of him stood his massive custom designed oak desk which was about as tidy as the shelves. Besides the laptop, a growing tower of unwashed coffee cups and swaths of ungraded exams, there was a curious assortment of limestone figurines from pre-Hellenic Crete, Ivory Demon masks from West Africa, Sumerian clay tablets and a whole lot of more or less unidentifiable curiosa that would cause any British Museum curator to salivate with envy. The actual available working space amounted to less than two eights of its total surface. He flicked his wrist and glanced at his watch, a Baume & Mercier Hampton gold edition, and combed through what little he had left of his thin grey hair with his fingers. -Exactly one hour until he would meet «them». Taking off his reading glasses he packed his laptop into its briefcase, pocketed his keys and headed for the door.

Stepping out of the universities main entrance the rain seemed to take a short break though the wind had picked up. It was surprisingly hot. The rapidly thickening cloud cover had turned from hues of light pastel via cobalt blue to ash grey in a manner of minutes. Metrology was certainly not his field but nothing about it felt natural. Anxiety mounting, he picked up his pace as he headed to Blindern subway station.

The few usually so precious moments during the familiar tube ride yielded no respite this evening. On the contrary, they evoked in his mind old and uncomfortable truths. That in his heart of hearts he felt nothing but contempt for those people. They were living reminders of everything that age and experience had proven to be short sighted, greed-driven and abased about the human condition.
Beyond this unbecoming animosity, lurked the undeniable fact that he had made them into a projected embodiment of his own shortcomings. Shortcomings that, despite his many accomplish-

ments he had never been fully able to face.

In an effort to regain his composure, Ystad decided to get off at Majorstua station. Hoping that the fresh air and beautiful scenery would put his mind at ease, he started making his way down toward the Vigeland sculpture park on foot. He passed the innocent looking statue of Sonja Henie with her tight-lipped Mona Lisa-like smile just as it started pouring down again and was about to cross the patio that led to the park's main entrance when he became aware of the unmistakeable presence of someone who, judging by the feelings intensity, certainly had attained the degree of Magus, if not higher.

«What's with you today good Professor? Do you feel... regret? »

The sentences didn't reach him in the form of sound waves generated by vibrating vocal cords setting tiny bones in his inner ear in motion. No, they were more akin to how someone suffering from untreated OCD or Schizophrenia would experience the full strength of their most tenacious of obsessive thoughts. -A high speed freight train of ideas that simply wouldn't let themselves be ignored. Ystad stopped in his tracks and gave them his full attention. They were neither baneful nor depressing in their emotional tonality, like he often had experienced during evocation of higher Demons. They did however carry with them the stable imprint of a relaxed yet frighteningly strong focus. Ystad turned in their general direction, walked off the pavement traversing a lawn strewn with glistening, freshly cut grass towards an unfamiliar grove of gigantic ash trees. There, in the middle of a small semicircle about 30 feet in front of him, his astral senses placed the origin of the signal. It seemed completely vacant save for an unorganised mess of dirty rags and flattened, whet cardboard boxes.

«Every single day!» He pulsed back «Yet it is our mistakes that provides the friction of our improvement! » There was a short pause as the tone of the «thought choir» darkened considerably; «Regret isn't a tool for self-improvement, it is a cage! And yours could the house the whole of this city!»
«That's exactly why I need to keep mindful of it!»
The words came bursting out of his mouth even though he hadn't meant to sever the telepathic connection. Ystad swore under his breath at how easily he had let himself be carried away by his emo-

tions, and for a short while the only response he got was the rustling of long dead leaves that seemed to dance in small vortexes
around his legs. A soundless rumbling escorted by a few palpable
tremors ran through the ground at that instant, then the heap of
garbage and filth seemed to vibrate until its undefinable layers of
cloth, plastic containers and cardboard just started ripping themselves apart revealing a puddle of inky black liquid through which
a tall, bony, almost hollow man floated up as if the worn-out blan-
kets and loose pieces of waste hid a secret tunnel leading straight
to the Abyss.

He was naked except for an old pair of Adidas shorts, and so dirty
it looked like he spent all his time digging graves with his bare
hands. Beneath all the grime and mould Ystad could barely make
out strange symbols covering every inch of his skin that certainly
didn't belong to any culture he knew of. -Personal sigils most
likely. Yet his eyes were clear as crystal, steel blue and held Ystad's
gaze in an iron grip.

Ystad examined the sensation without blinking an eye. The older
man's attention was like a force of nature. -A sun whose circumstances had no choice but to let themselves be defined by the shear
clarity of its presence.

The raggedy fellow measured him up and down with unbridled
contempt. «So, you think you can withstand its influence? That
you are free? -Incorruptible? -Your stuck in Her net already» Ystad
couldn't help but follow his stare and look down at himself. His
shiny Italian shoes, the sharpness of the press in his pants, his
English tweed jacket, the Armani shirt, the silk handkerchief, and
the watch he so cherished, before looking back up at the unkept
renouncer. Yes, it was all true. He felt entitled to certain extrava-
gances. During the 25 years of his very exemplary career, he had
developed expensive tastes and knew how to indulge in life's
many pleasures. -Who wouldn't have?

«What did they promise you? Fame? Fortune? Respect? Revela-
tions? Redemption? You will revel in it all while your hands are
stained with the worst of offences!»

«A chance to make a difference, nothing more» Ystad bit back. The
Ascetic slacked a bit of his mental grip. «What difference? The
pride of the beast of burden? The aches bought with meaningless
chores? You will fail» he said with a hint of genuine sadness in his
voice.

19

«So, what would you have me do? Sell all my belongings and join you here? »

The old man smiled. "What do you mean here? I'm in the middle of Reality. You are off somewhere else. It is folly to listen to someone who refuses to listen himself. Go to them and meet your fate, fool. We had such hopes for you"

«Me too...» Ystad said and turned towards the park. He could feel the old man's stare boring into his back, but he kept on walking.

It was only after he came out of the little grove and stepped through the main entrance that Ystad became aware of how few people were in the park at this hour. He could barely make out some silhouettes at the outskirts, but that was about it. He picked up his pace a little and headed for the Monolith. He started upon the stairs leading to the podium still gripped in the familiar feeling of solitude while pondering the complete lack of visitors in the middle of the tourist season.

There was something else there though. Transparent, and surely invisible to non-Magicians, there seemed to be veil-like Astral cobwebs fluttering, like raggedy, wind torn flags left by some bygone, polar explorer stretching between the granite statues. Sinew-like strands glowing white-green, expanded not from the 56 feet high crowning achievement of Vigeland's Genius but seemingly from a rather small, almost unnoticeable statue of an adolescent girl standing entwined in the coils of a sleeping Dragon. On second thought he wasn't so sure the Dragon had any power over the innocent looking youth at all. Her posture and the way the dragon lay coiled at her feet told a different story than his flimsy first impressions. She looked fearless, bordering on commanding with her regal attitude and focused eyes as if she knew he was there and kept on looking straight through him. Intuitively Ystad turned around as if to discern the object of her attention. That's when he saw it. The sky had now turned dark red and the cloud cover seemed to rebel against the winds. It started churning in a gigantic spiral whose epicentre seemed to be just a few hundred yards to the east of his position. Ystad turned his head and scrutinised the granite face of the little girl. But to no avail. She still kept her silence.

The course laid out by the statue had gotten him out of the park now and into the forest area around and between some of the wealthiest houses in Oslo. Rain-soaked branches embraced him and a carpet of leaves from last year's autumn that somehow retained their sparkle made the circumstances even more bewildering. He followed a small brook guided by far between lampposts and the faint light from impressive looking villas. He could feel he was getting closer now. Most of the villas he was passing although they tried to outdo each other in luxurious gimmicks and overpriced equipment, still emitted impressions of ordinary families with ordinary problems. The building he was heading for, did not.

The track suddenly angled sharply to the left and took him over a simple wooden bridge followed by a steep flight of stairs. On top of them, flanked by a pair of Hellhound-like Gargoyles were lampposts in wrought black iron emitting a greenish light. Other than the colour there was another thing he found perplexing. There were no insects in their vicinity. Absolutely none.

From the top of the stairs the narrow track widened into a well-kept gravel-filled avenue flanked by tall chestnut trees on either side leading up to a spacious courtyard. In the middle of it, a richly decorated circular fountain with rows of luxury cars parked on either side. Among them he could make out three red Ferraris, numerous silver Rolls Royce's, a lime green Koenigsegg Jesko and even a noble looking 18th century horse carriage whose driver still manned his post decked out in matching costume. Stairs of white marble led from the courtyard up into an upper terrace directly in front of the main entrance to what could only be described as a rather annoying cross between a German castle and an upper-class villa in the Norwegian Jugend style of the 1920s. Beneath the archway of the enormous double doors, he could just make out the silhouette of a woman about his own age clad in a champagne-coloured evening gown with matching upper arm length gloves and a sparkling tiara. She greeted each guest with a courteous bow even though it was obvious from the body language of those waiting in line to be admitted into the main building that she was the ranking attendant. Between the guests, carrying trays of refreshments and attending to their needs, were at least two dozen servants easily recognisable in blue and white uniforms.

Ystad stalked over the meticulously trimmed lawn in the direction of some rather curious looking bushes. They had been trimmed to resemble three animals rendered in lifelike detail. One was a lion sitting on its hind legs holding a ball formed sceptre in its right paw. The other two a swan with its wings outstretched carrying a jewel necklace around its long neck and a mean looking and crowned boar lumped on a kingly throne. Another thing Ystad found curious was that they were arranged in an equilateral triangle with each animal looking inwards towards the centre. The swan occupied the uppermost angle, closest to the grotesque castle.

At the other end of the huge garden stood several smaller buildings. Lodgings of the service personnel no doubt. He had been expressly instructed that he was not to use the main entrance but one of the fire exits, courtesy of the many dignitaries that would be in attendance this evening. That had stung his professional pride a little but the compensation he'd been promised for two hours' worth of private lecturing amounted to just over three months' worth of what the faculty paid him, so he hadn't raised any objections.

Turning the south-eastern corner, he was greeted by a smart looking young man with meticulously groomed sand blond hair in a freshly pressed servants uniform complete with white gloves. He seemed rather anxious. Almost tiptoeing around while Ystad walked over.
«Professor Ystad! How good of you to come. Right this way please. There's not a moment to lose.» «You all seem rather busy today? I think I can find my way to the second-floor library if you have other duties to attend to» Ystad said to the servants back as he rushed towards the fire exit. «There's been a change of plans» the boy said without looking over his shoulder. I won't be showing you to the library». «Where to then?» Ystad could feel he was starting to sweat. If it was one thing he disliked, it was last minute changes to plans. «To the forbidden door» replied the youth. «I really can't tell you much more».

They were now in a broad hallway with a tall ceiling. Although he could hear lots of activity on the upper floors they were completely alone. Snippets of conversation and laughter some whose voices seemed faintly familiar like that of retired politicians and over the hill TV hosts, carried down through open windows and elevator shafts. They passed a long row of large paintings. Portraits mostly of...

«Ah, here we are» His guide had so suddenly and unexpectedly stopped that Ystad bumped into him. They were standing in front of a large wooden door painted all black with a brass plate in its centre shaped like an octagon. It didn't have any script on it just the engraved image of a burning Sun with eight wavy rays, each of which terminated in its corresponding angle.

The servant produced a large ornate key from one of his pockets and put it into a hole in the middle of the sun which Ystad hadn't noticed at all. «This is as far as I'm aloud to go. You will find written instructions waiting for you in the dressing room».
«The what?» Ystad stammered. «And please hurry up, will you? They'll kill me if I keep you any longer. Best of luck!» And with that his escort hurried down the corridor. Ystad was about to shout after him but he didn't want to draw attention to himself. Taking a few deep breaths, he pushed the door open and stepped inside its velvety shadow.

Ystad fumbled for a light switch unsuccessfully. His hands did however locate a rail. Easing his feet slowly forward it became apparent that he was standing on the top of a spiral staircase. As his eyes adjusted to the gloom, he could barely make out a faint light source deep beneath him. Wall hung chandeliers by the looks of it. Clutching the rail, he started descending towards that light. As he got closer it looked as if someone was holding out their arm, beckoning him to come closer with their index finger. «Hello! I demand an explanation! » he yelled. Dead silent. He completed the last few rungs just as the chandelier came fully into view. There was no person at the end of the arm. Rather the chandelier itself was the arm. A blue-white flame was hovering directly above its palm and its shoulder socket protruded from the walls surface without any visible mounting. It hung beside an arch leading into a room that was much better lit though still only by candlelight. Ystad walked cautiously in, still expecting to find someone who could explain this strange turn of events. The room was furnished with bookcases on every wall. To his right was another arch leading into what looked like a small antechamber. He swore he could make out a silhouette of someone in there. He grabbed one of the candles and walked over «Excuse me! Could you please tell me what the hell I'm supposed to be doing? » The silhouette didn't move an inch and pretty soon the candlelight revealed that he had been talking to a full-size male manikin. It wore what looked to be a blaspheming mockery of a catholic bishop's regalia consisting of a burgundy red Alb with gold trimmings, a dark green cape, some comfy looking slippers and most peculiar of all, a large wooden mask. It was painted with gold leaf but displayed absolutely zero human features. Instead of a face it had deeply cut furrows writhing into a vortex that was spinning in counterclockwise direction. In its very centre sat a crouching spider rendered in excruciating detail. A small cream coloured card had been pinned to the cape at the chest. Ystad had to lean in pretty close to discern what it said. Three simple words: «Put this on».

There was something undeniably alluring with this whole situation. At the same time his sense of reason was screaming warnings at maximum volume inside his head. The conflict of interest made him dizzy. Surely, he could at least take a closer look at that curious mask? -For professional reasons of course. Slowly and carefully, he lifted it off the velvety manikin head and held it up close. Wasn't there a better light source around here somewhere? That's when he heard it. It sounded like stone gnashing against stone combined with the light scraping of chalk on an old-fashioned blackboard. Instantly he could feel a draft through the room and a drop of temperature. For a few moments all was silence and he sighed in relief. Then he became aware of a humming sound.

It was barely audible. He could just make out the sibilants in the beginning. But it seemed to come from what he had thought was a closet. He took a few daring steps forward still holding the grotesque mask in his right hand feeling his way forward with the left. Everything around him was grey, colourless, featureless in the gloom. Especially now that he blocked what little light emerged from the eerie torch with his back. The doors of the cupboard were moving ever so slightly by the energy of the draft. As his eyes became more adjusted to the dark it seemed to open up totally just as he came up in front of it as if it was beckoning him to enter. Ystad peered inside. The smell of moss clad stonework and old cellars greeted his nose. This was no cupboard at all but a really old secret passage. The brickwork and cobblestone suggested its construction to be before the great fire of 1624 after which the Danish-Norwegian King Christian IV had ordered the city to be rebuilt closer to Bjørvika. He was about to cross the threshold when the humming returned and unexpectedly warped into a whooping crescendo. It wasn't humming at all but chanting. Ystad's professional curiosity slipped from his mind to give way to a much more primitive sensation. He felt exposed. He wanted to run up the stairs and out of this accursed complex damn the money and his reputation. Words bore into his mind like a drill. «Do you feel... regret? » -No, he would not give into fear, but he could hide in plain sight. He looked over his shoulder at the dark silhouette of the manikin and started undoing his belt buckle and opening his shirt.

A few moments later he had the full get up more or less on. It fitted him rather well. Bowing low he made his way through the cupboard his hand again finding a sturdy rail on the right-hand side. The chanting rose and fell in gyrating, unexpected turns as if a group of contemporary performance artists rehearsed for some avant garde play down there in the dark. Suddenly Ystad could feel it becoming brighter. He still couldn't make out much through the narrow slits cut in at eye level in the furrows of the mask, but its edges had become less gloomy. After a few more paces the voices started echoing with the reverb of a large subterranean cavern and he could make out the rustling of cloaks and the patting sound of bare feet on stone. Some utterly disorienting soundtrack seemed to be playing in the background and the rustling of feet multiplied fast arguably covering a large area judging by their ambience. The light dimmed again to be extinguished completely leaving everyone in the same all-enveloping Darkness. The railings on the wall came to its end at that same instant, and Ystad had the distinct feeling that he was shuffling forward on some malevolent stage involuntarily playing the part of himself at the leisure of cruel gods.

Stumbling forward in the long skirt of the Alb, he automatically felt before him with his left arm and caught something sharp, hard, and cold. It was clearly of either metal or stone but he retracted like he had accidentally stumbled into a sleeping bear. There was an undeniable exchange there and his mind felt the touch of an intelligence older than the stars. As he recoiled it was as if his whole nervous system had been plugged into a nuclear power plant of spiritual energy and all his magical faculties were suddenly sharper and more powerful than they ever had been.

THOMAS KARLSSON PH.D

He still couldn't see much but the outlines of his surroundings had become more pronounced like edges in the negative of a photograph. Moreover, the thing that he had bumped into was but a leg of a gargantuan statue of a grotesque Spider-human hybrid with the upper body of a voluptuous female where the spiders head would normally be. He was presently standing in its shadow near an elevated dais cut out of natural stalactites that had been chiselled to a resemble some diabolical altar. Hellish vents to either side of it seemed to emit a sulphuric gas that had been enkindled and now blazed with a greenish unnatural flame. Their flickering sparkle spawned countless short-lived shadows dancing all over the huge spider, like bewildering strobe lights at a rave party from some lunatic acid-heads darkest dream. The spider statue that undoubtedly weighed several hundred tonnes seemed to hang suspended in the air save for a couple of its legs barely touching the ceiling. Directly beneath it and in front of Ystad, a deep gorge effectively cut the raised area he found himself, on from the rest of the isle-like cavern. He could glimpse the dark cloaks of many participants on the other side. Everyone had hoods drawn up around their faces save one.

Instead of a black cloak she wore an all-white, body hugging costume that seemed to have feathers attached to it. Brightly coloured makeup gave the impression of a Ballerina straight out of «Swan Lake» Even in the gloom and behind the heavy mask he could feel their eyes meeting.
It was Her.

In a flash the whole subterranean theatre faded away and the two of them was transported back to that fateful morning of September '93 he had fought so hard to erase from his memory. He had just been a junior researcher back then barely into his post doc program. They had never been formerly introduced but according to the hushed gossip in the cafeteria prior to his lecture, there was an Austrian Academic of some repute visiting the university that day. This someone was supposedly heiress to a great aristocratic house that stretched its pedigree well beyond the glory days of the Austrian-Hungarian Empire. According to Mr Vinje, head of the Mathematics faculty and the biggest gossiper this side of the Caledonian Orogeny, she had recently married the former

WWII hero, industrial magnate, and shipyard owner Jan Christian Hauge who at the time must have been twice her age. Hauge had (as if his earlier accomplishments weren't enough) spent most of the yuppy eighties establishing himself as a looming presence on every board of Directors in the Scandinavian shipping industry. By the early nineties he had become somewhat of a recluse only accessible to the uppermost strata of society, said to function as a private advisor to certain members of the Ministry of Defence and select Arctic research groups as well as multiple Royal families. This same Hauge was one of UIO`s most generous benefactors, a patron of the Arts and a well-known collector of occult artefacts and manuscripts.

That morning she had apparently flown in by private jet exclusively to sit front row on one of his first lectures on the custom of human sacrifice in Scandinavian bronze age cultures, the theme of his PhD thesis. This had struck Ystad as rather odd since it had never occurred that an insignificant junior like him had visitors from universities abroad on such a low-key event. As barely conscious students started shuffling out of the aula, she had walked towards him slowly with a ballroom dancers grace and nailed him to the spot with her gleaming emerald eyes, while explaining how she had, together with some other well-off people on the continent, recently created a trust for the sole purpose of providing funding for research projects in a whole list of very specific and rather narrow fields of study. During the conversation Ystad was struck with the level of detailed knowledge this enigmatic stunner possessed about his doctoral research.

She was of slender athletic build, quite tall, broad shouldered and endowed with cheek bones that look like they were chiselled out of white marble. She had worn a loose-fitting black knee length silk dress with no bra underneath. Matching black pumps and a small strapless handbag tucked under her left arm completed the Bond femme fatale/ Noir actress look. Her wavy blond hair was cut short and styled firmly backward. Aside from an eyeliner that accentuated her big almond shaped eyes, she wore very modest make up. Clearly, she was very aware of the fact that she didn't really need any.

Her classic Northern European beauty aside there was something else that almost made it uncomfortable to be in her presence. She emitted a kind of magnetic confidence that bordered on the predatory. It shot out in every direction and seemed to fill the whole auditorium judging by the faces of the few students who had lingered behind. All without batting an eyelash. Her face was almost blank betraying no emotion at all. This «inverted star power» was in the process of reversing the queue of people trying to get to their lunch breaks as students in the hallway started catching on to the fact that something extraordinary was taking place inside the auditorium.

At that moment she had stopped mid-sentence, looked briefly over her left shoulder at the young men trying to pick their jaws of the floor, then treated Ystad to a short nod before producing a thick, expensive looking business card from the handbag. She'd held it out towards him between two meticulously manicured fingernails and dropped it into his hand as he was about to take it. With that, his audience was over. The throng of students, teachers and hang-arounds had parted before her like the Red Sea before Moses as she made her way to the exit. She must have been well out in the parking lot before anyone dared a sigh of relief. Even after that Ystad found that he hadn't moved an inch. He had just kept staring down into his cupped palms. At the cream white watermarked card bound in intrinsically stylised Gothic letters which formed only two short sentences:

«Vera von List,
Direktor der Nerþuz Gesellschaft»

Some weeks later, just when he had managed to forget about the whole incident, he had found an envelope in his mailbox at work of the same colour and texture. Inside where more praise for his research and information on projects being formulated within the same area and instructions on how to contact the project management. To his astonishment he was being invited to join as a permanent retainer. It was signed by some of the foremost experts in his field. Professors at Oxford, Yale, Amsterdam and Stockholm to name but a few. The envelope also contained a contract that should he accept detailed the substantial compensation that went into the package. On top of the handsome fee, it promised access to some of the most coveted collections of manuscripts and locations of study in the world.

Ystad involuntarily shook his head and the weight and reality of the morbid thing he wore over his face drew him back to the present, the underground hall and the absence of light.

Looking ahead, the congregation on the other side of the precipice had lit torches now. The von List woman was still staring straight at him and seemed to try to force him out of his reverie with quiet though still commanding looks, like a soufflé cueing in a derailed actor. Guided by a strange impulse he shuffled up the few flights of stairs towards the dais. Its flames had died down now somewhat and he felt a little reassured by the conviction that he was less visible up there. The chanting and wooing died completely down, and the enormous chamber fell into complete silence.

«Brothers and sisters!» Her voice reverberated through the hall. «Let us hear the Arachne Invocation!

Once again, she nodded in Ystad's direction and now he felt the palpable attention of everyone bearing down on him. Without really thinking about it he started feeling for his reading glasses which he evidently had left behind in the dressing room. He found something else though. On the inside of his cape stylishly sewn perpendicular to the seem there was a long narrow pocket of some kind. The index finger of his right hand found it entirely by mistake and inside it a roll of stiff light weight paper. As he pulled it out it gave off the same silvery luminescence as the cobwebs he had experienced by the Monolith earlier that day. What's more, the text it contained was somehow perfectly readable even in the dancing shadows and without his glasses. Over the top of the scroll the woman in the swan costume seemed more content as she turned to her congregation.

«Master of Tooth, bring forth the candidates!»

Faintly he could see beneath the lit torches that the throng of cloaks slowly parted in the midst and that four naked individuals, three men and one woman, was roughly showed forward by a tall muscular man that was also naked save for a hideous mask shaped like the head of a wild boar, complete with open maw and tusks drenched in some red liquid.

The four shuffled awkwardly forward the best they could dragging their left leg behind them a little as if with a limp.

As they lined up in front of their swan-like queen it became evident that they wore a shackle around their left ankles. Ystad hurriedly peered down at the strange scroll in his hands just as the commanding presence of the Swan Priestess turned in his direction again. Knowing that he had no choice Ystad started to read out loud:

«Great Mother Arachne!» To his immediate bafflement his voice was carried swiftly by the reverb of the large cavern even though he hadn't tried to speak particularly loudly and despite the added hinderance of the mask. Hidden spotlights of red light were gradually turned on and revealed the huge spider goddess in all her stark majesty. Its posture was incredibly lifelike and gave the impression that it had just stalked its way through a hidden rent in reality. Some of its legs touched the ceiling, others the walls and a one or two the floor which gave off the impression of floating weightless regardless of its enormous bulk.
The effect it had on the guests which must have been oblivious to it up to this moment must have been one of fear-tinged Sublimity. The Egregoric atmosphere devoured their enthusiasm greedily and hardened to an almost fog like consistency as Ystad continued:

«Mistress of Time and Space, seamstress of the Cosmic tapestry, Devourer of Worlds and Guardian of the Secrets of the Void!
Let those who lack the strength to free themselves from self-chosen limitations be caught in your net for all eternity!
But let the Elect drink of your poisoned chalice and be reborn by your forbidden knowledge and elevated to your compassionless and dimensionless Order!
As the planets dance around the sun, and the axil is ever the centre of its wheel, are you encroached and watchful from the centre of circumstances.

Unmoved, unchanging, tireless and infinity patient

Until the end of the All!»

«Until the end of the All!» the congregation roared

URD! -«Urd!»

KALI! «Kali!»

ARACHNE! «Arachne!"

NERTHUS! «Nerthus!»

SATARIEL! «Satariel!" the congregation answered, and the echoes of each call seemed to reverberate endlessly passed the stone walls of the enormous chamber.

Ystad looked over the scroll just as the von List woman nodded in his direction. Torches had been lit on a small platform hanging over the precipice and now the hog-headed man had unshackled his female prisoner while the swan clad high priestess led her by the hand up a few steps to the top of the platform.

«The die is cast, are you ready to surrender yourself to the Weaver of Destinies? »
The young woman managed a slight nod as she completed the final step.
Her slender form bathed in the cold light of a single bright beam trained directly at her head. «Then go to her! Yelled the Swan-clad priestess. The girl hesitated, clearly out of her element after which the priestess grabbed her by the neck and unceremoniously showed her over the edge. Her high-pitched scream rolled through the cavernous hall before it too seemed to disappear in the now rapidly thickening mist.
The next candidate seemed a bit bolder and more jumped off the platform without any help from the hight priestess. It occurred to Ystad then that there were no sound of impact of any kind. Surely, they had a safety net installed?
One candidate to go but even before he got on to the platform Ystad could tell that something bad was about to happen. From his pale wrinkled body and the way he moved, it was clear that he had to be in his eighties at least. There was a short exchange where it seemed that the ever so stern mistress of ceremonies faltered in her conviction as if the old man knew something that she hadn't planned on sharing with anyone. Their eyes met for only a couple of moments but Ystad could tell that to the two of them it might as well have been an eternity. The Swan averted her eyes. «You were supposed to find me the Lion!» The old man said, clearly out of script. Bewilderment and confusion started to eat at the attend-ees as it became apparent that the beautiful blond on the platform wasn't in control anymore.
«I told you to…» The old man was just about to finish his sentence when he seemed to lose his footing. Before anyone could react, he fell backwards over the pit, not flailing his arms or screaming at

all.

The high priestess however, she screamed on top of her voice. «Jaaaan!» This time there were a loud whet crack from the dark pit. «Fuck him» Vera cleared her throat and adjusted her get up while trying to act like nothing had happened. «Now where was I» she said more to herself than anyone else.

«The Weaver of Fates has made her will known to us and our intrepid candidates has put their very souls in her net of cruelty. May the worthy be elevated!»

«May the worthy be elevated» the congregation muttered not quite in unison. Their restlessness was palpable now.

«May the unworthy be crushed in Kali's mortar and be ground into the dust from which a new world shall recreate itself! » The attendees seemed even more uneasy now and there was no automatic answer to the passage. von List scrutinised the throng of people around her in the torch light «I said may the...»

The rumbling was deafening. Ystad couldn't place it accurately in the poor light but it sounded like a crack was opening up somewhere in the hall. The gargantuan spider statue swayed for a nauseating moment and then just seemed to come off its hinges crashing into the platform beneath taking much of the cliff edge with it. Pure panic erupted. People trampled and clawed at each other to get to the emergency exits through whirling clouds of debris. Screams and shouts continued up the corridors as new fissures were spreading throughout natural bedrock and manmade fundaments as well.

At last silence settled in and Ystad became conscious of himself again. Cold sweat ran down his face as he became aware of the soreness of his neck from the weight of the mask. He was alone. Well, not quite alone.

The sensation had been primarily mental ever since entering the building but had by now taken on a clinging heaviness similar to having innumerable gallons of sea water over you during deep sea diving. An overwhelming need to take the mask off from not being able to breath shot up in his consciousness like a supersonic projectile, and during a few hazy microseconds his animal nature at last overtook that all important self-discipline he had honed over so many years and grown so very attached to. His hands held the grotesque, helmet-like thing in front of him before his mind could register that it had actually come off his face. He let out a sigh of relief. At the same time, the temperature dropped.

That's when they appeared.
Three luminescent white Spiders with a shimmering unstable coarseness to them like a TV image with bad reception. Ystad made his hands into fists and compressed his focus to the sharpness of a scalpel. They crawled into his centre of attention all the same with the effortless grace that natural spiders utilise while entering a derelict barn with a crack in a wall. A shadow behind him caressed his spine with pulsating undulations of temperature and tactility transporting him to his dearest childhood memory.
-Lying just at the edge of the surf on a sandy beach with the deep blue of a cloudless sky above him. -The cool caress of the waves and the coarseness of sand and seashells as they withdrew, the cries of seagulls, the wetness of his bathing trunks and the laughter of a group of girls a little older than himself. All of it had coalesced into a perfect moment he had wished would never die. He had wanted to stay there indefinitely and never grow up. -To be in a sense, its willing prisoner.

The teasing female voices from the memory erupted at full volume in his mind. In one instant as the flirtatious self-imposing laughter of a manipulative 13-year-old, in the next the sympathetic straightforwardness of a 33-year-old who knows that you cannot defend against the common sense of her argument, and beneath it all, rolling like an unstoppable echo out of the epicentre of the Void itself, throat splitting cries of sheer anguish heralding the birth-pains of the Universe and the heart wrenching wisdom of timeless Feminine Mysteries.

The shimmering white spiders moved towards him soundlessly from the other side of the hall. One moved upside down over the ceiling, another hung from a single leg before disappearing only to reappear just a couple of yards from him. The third sat perfectly still in the angle between wall and ceiling. Ystad instinctively covered his ears as the sound reminiscent of a large sheath of fabric being slowly ripped in two announced the full presence of the First Goddess.
A hole in reality yawned towards him like a never-ending tunnel and from it floated black snowflakes carried on imperceptible winds from uncreated dimensions.

The bewildering touch at his back that still fluctuated between warmth and coldness, softness and clawing hardness, coalesced at a point on his left shoulder blade and chose for itself the shape of a female hand. The contact point felt like an umbilical cord anchoring him to the very centre of absolute reality. Ystad had to muster his last reserves of energy just to keep from losing consciousness and control of his bodily functions.

«Vai-Karana» whispered the female voices. A graven feeling of great transparency spread to his every cell, laying bare every secret and bit of shame he had ever harboured.

To his surprise it seemed to lend extra luminescence to his mind as well providing a vantage point for self-observation he had previously only glimpsed in short moments of the most refined Gnosis.

Time and space fought themselves in violent death spasms until they finally shrivelled off completely, like a serpent´s cast off skin. He tried to feel the ache in his neck and legs. He wasn't quite sure if he had a body anymore. In front of him, if it indeed made any sense to think of any direction as something apart from any other, reality folded in on itself like a glistening syrupy cone before disappearing as if swallowed by some cosmic vacuum cleaner that took his complete field of vision with it.

The white spiders were the only things that gave any continuity to the experience. They squatted, crawled, and hung from surfaces that wasn't there but all the same confirmed that he at least retained some of his memory. The hand at his shoulder stalked over his chest and a voluptuous female body hugged him tightly from behind. She was a hot as lava and at the same time cold as ice. The maddening nothing in front of him unfurled in yet more layers, like the petals of a Lotus flower filmed in long exposure unto judgement day and beyond.

Becoming, growth, decay, and death into new becoming. Everything seemed to evolve independently of but at the same time synchronised in minute detail with millions of pulsating objects. Some were repulsive and confusing. Others intensely beautiful and fascinating.

For an instant they twinkled and unfurled themselves before him like a swarm of shiny lidless eyes before expanding and congealing into a massive sinew-like tapestry as time and distance again

found some resemblance of themselves. A fleshy, burgundy coloured carpet knitted itself together beneath his feet as bundles of
bulging arteries rose up from it to form thick trunks vaguely in
the shape of trees.

At a hazy horizon, a cold bluish light seemed to be dawning.
Next, another layer of detail covered the meaty surroundings and
came into focus as a windswept heath surrounded by flat grass-
lands. He was lying by a marshy pond close to a small cliff adorned
by a majestic Yew tree. Chills ran up his body. He was whet. A mer-
ciless wind cut through to the bone and, as he picked himself up
looking down at himself, he became aware of the fact that he had
no clothes on. Moreover, there seemed to be the rustling sounds of
capes and simple percussion instruments behind him. He stopped
and turned around. There were a whole procession of people
watching him intently. They were mostly garbed in simple tunics
and shawls. Some were naked. As he faced them, they fanned out
in a half circle silently. Behind them there was a simple wooden
cart drawn by a white bull. Tight lipped and staring they started
to advance. Ystad stepped backward, keeping his distance until he
had waded knee deep into the ice-cold pond. Its murky bottom felt
unsure and slimy. Was this another vision?
He tried to get his bearings. There was something undoubtedly
familiar with the area. Looking around there were no landmarks
that he recognised, but he was sure he had visited this place all
the same. His onlookers seemed to grow impatient with him. An
old man, thin and sinewy wearing nothing but a loin cloth broke
ranks and started to make his way through the tall weeds by the
pond carrying a tall wooden staff. His body was covered in a myr-
iad of swirly symbols painted in bright red. Ochre Ystad guessed.
The man came up in front of him silently. Staring straight into his
eyes he held his staff in his right hand shaking it a little to indicate
its significance. With his left he drew a highly polished blade of
bronze and held that outwards as well.
The bearded fellow shook both items once more. Ystad could feel
he was sinking further down into the mud of the pond. What
did this all mean? He was certain he was supposed to remember
something. The murky sediment on the bottom of the pond seem
to suck him downwards and he just realised he had slid down
to his thighs. At the same time, a terrible realisation was about
to be born in his mind something he fought hard not to see. He

knew these people; he knew this place. He knew the ache in his shoulders. And it had nothing to do with the terrible mask he had been wearing. It was from carrying the Idol. The old man held the bronze dagger hilt first in front of him as Ystad finally came to a startling realisation. This was his Work. This was Egtved, Denmark 3500 years ago. Despite his pretending otherwise his whole life had been stuck here ever since accepting that damn grant. This was here. He had always been here.

The old man shook the hand holding the dagger one final time. He had been permitted a glimpse of the great Mother Nerthus and was now expected to die with his knowledge. By ritual suicide. Meeting the bearded man's gaze, he gripped the hilt of the dagger and held the blade to his throat. Sliding the blade across didn't produce any pain. It produced sounds. Sounds of laughter and the surging surf.

THE MONSTER OF CONCORD

By Leo Holmes

Dear Mr. Holmes,

I was born in Concord, New Hampshire, to a moderately rich couple of Franco-American ancestry. I don't remember them though. My mother died of liver cancer, I guess, or something alike, developed as a consequence of her Porphyria. Porphyria cutanea tarda. I was raised by my maternal aunt, Charlize, who told me my father committed suicide just a few months after the death of my mother. He couldn't bear the burden.

Although I lacked nothing in economic terms, my childhood was not exactly joyful or easy; I don't have good memories. Charlize, who is fortunately dead now, was a fervent Christian fundamentalist with very little tolerance towards anything; not to say no tolerance at all. She used to say that it was lack of faith that killed my parents, the lack of religious zeal. As a result, my childhood was obviously not like that of the other boys of the 80's in my area. I couldn't go out and play with them, I couldn't even play alone. All I was allowed to do was go to school, read at home —preferably the Bible or another book carefully selected by her— and to use my father's telescope when the weather permitted. The stars were my only friends. I couldn't stay long with them though, I had to sleep early. She was intolerably rigid, abusive, the monster. I secretly nicknamed her "The Monster".

We lived alone, the two of us, in my father's enormous house. Huge, full of emptied, dusty rooms, humid—mouldy is the word—and dark; it was frighteningly dark. Charlize preferred the light of candles, she used to say electricity "is the Devil's master plan for the end times". The smell of melting wax was nauseating. Besides, the shadows cast by the flickering flames would give life to bizarre, eerie creatures in my imagination. That is, I suppose it was my imagination; kids have a fruitful imagination, you know. This whole scenario, I think, was the greatest reason for my childhood nightmares. I was plagued with nightmares. I mean, my waking life was a nightmare as a whole, but nothing compares to my nightly terrors at the time.

I used to hear steps just above my room; sometimes I heard voices whispering my name. I am surprised that I never pissed myself. Perhaps it was because I was more afraid of Charlize's punishments than of ghosts. I remember once telling her that I heard the aforementioned steps from above my room—from the attic—upon which she became furious, physically chastised me and made me kneel on the corn. I have a cauliflowered ear, but it was not from jujitsu, it was Charlize. She also used to beat me with a wooden ruler for everything she considered misbehaviour. Fuck, I thought I would never survive her. I was relieved that Mr. Gagnon intervened on a few occasions. He was an old gardener, the only stranger who came to our property every fifteen days or so. He seemed to like me, always trying somehow to protect me from that bitch. I heard while at school at the time that his only granddaughter passed away in the previous year, a victim of meningitis. Maybe this explained his despondent atmosphere. He was mostly quiet, but when he talked to me while I observed him trimming trees or caring for the roses, he often spoke of what seemed to be spiritual matters in gardening metaphors. Something like "flowers are the angels of this realm" or "plants are the only truly charitable beings you'll ever find in your life".

One day I told him that I heard steps from the attic and also strange noises from the kitchen; I said that I thought the house was haunted. Instead of reprehending me or dismissing my appeal as a childish nonsense, he gave me a freshly collected white rose and told me to pray for the angels while holding it whenever I felt haunted again. I still have it. It never worked, though. On one occasion, I guess I was thirteen at the time, he accidentally disclosed that my father hung himself in that very attic. According to him, it was there that my father spent most of his time after my mother's death. Mr. Gagnon also liked to watch the stars; we often talked about astronomy.

One night I was in my room watching the stars with my father's telescope, when Charlize came in with a bad mood—with no apparent reason, as was frequent—and told me to go to sleep. I begged her for a few extra minutes, but her response was to slap the telescope out of my hands. Shocked, I ran to bed and covered myself under the sheets, after which she forced me to say the prayer. I waited a little while after she left the room and quietly slipped out of the bed to check on the telescope; the lenses were broken. I was immediately depressed; the only gates leading me out of this awful reality were now forever shut. My only toy was broken, the sole thing that connected me to my deceased father and to my only friends, the stars. I wished Charlize was dead.

After that, I spent the nights looking at the sky with naked eyes for a week or so, trying to reconnect to my distant friends. In one way or another, some of them seemed to understand me as I spoke to them; they seemed to reply back. They communicated through twinkles. But I missed using the telescope, it shortened the distance between us. Then it occurred to me that my father might have a spare pair of lenses in the attic; after all, it was there that his things were kept, I guessed—where he spent most of his time after my mother's death. He must have a kit or something. But Charlize kept the attic locked, she would never allow me to go in there.

On the following morning, Mr. Gagnon came to sweep the leaves and to care for the garden and, as usual, I came to watch him. I told him Charlize had broken my telescope and that I felt even more alone since then; at night, in a haunted house. I asked him if he could lend me a flashlight, so I could feel safer in the dark. "Of course, kid", he said, "but 'she' must never know, otherwise she'll be mad at me". Another fifteen torturous days had passed until Mr. Gagnon met me again; he brought me the flashlight, concealed in a folded shirt. I was careful enough not to allow her to see either the shirt or the flashlight. But I had specific plans for that flashlight beyond keeping me safe at night; I knew nothing could. So I waited for Charlize to go to sleep, struggling against sleep myself, and then put my plan in practice.

The idea of trying to enter the attic alone scared the shit out of me, but it seemed to be the only chance of having my telescope fixed. I knew there was a key box on the kitchen wall; the key had to be there. Being as silent as I could, walking on the tips of my toes, I went down the stairs with the flashlight in one hand and Mr. Gagnon's now depetalled rose stalk on the other—as a talisman—fervently hoping not to see a spook. The smell of recently extinguished candles still plagued the air as I crossed the living room; I had a strange feeling of being watched as I was doing it. Focusing on my breath, I hoped not to hear the whispers that called my name. I finally made it to the kitchen and saw the key box. I wished there were fewer keys.

As Charlize was not much taller than I was, I supposed the less-used keys were at the top; this would also be logical in case she organized the key box in accordance to the house's disposition: front door, kitchen and barn at the bottom, the other rooms in the middle to top and so on. She was very methodical, a total control freak. Consequently, she was also very predictable. I was left with the three topmost keys, one of which appeared to be too "modern" for the attic door. I grabbed the remaining two then I made my way to the attic. Careful not to make a noise, I tested the keys, one of which fitted. My excitement now exceeded my fear. I slipped my way into the attic, climbing the few steps of the stairs leading to it.

It was colder there, mouldier; the place obviously hadn't been cleaned in a long time and everything was covered in sheets, bringing my fear back to its place—the first place. The whole scene gave me the creeps. There was too much to explore in one single night and I knew I didn't have much time, so I started to scan the place. I saw many paintings, some covered, others not; I thought they were painted by my father, at least it appeared to be his name in the signature. One of them showed a shadowy ship in the middle of a tempest—dark, gloomy, chaotic. Looking back, I think it expressed my father's spiritual pains: anxiety, restlessness, uncertainty, his will to die.

There were also four or five dusty bookcases in which books shared space with glass jars filled with God-knows-what and various small metallic and stone figurines, mostly bizarre zoomorphic creatures resembling a few inhabitants of my nightmares. Leaning against one of the bookcases was a damaged cello; I never heard my father play, perhaps it was my mother's. The wind was making creepy noises; one window was broken, the shards were still there. I felt I heard a whisper calling my name, curiosity conquered fear. It came from a heavy desk near that broken window. Below the dust-ridden sheet that covered it, there were a few papers with engineering drawings, and pens and pencils spread across it. There was also a medium-sized wooden box; I knew from my heart the whisper came from it.

The moment I set my eyes on it, I was paralyzed; it had exquisite drawings burned on it. I fell in love with it immediately; at that moment, I didn't even remember what I was looking for. There was no more attic, no Charlize, no house, there was only that box. I can't express in words how much it attracted me; it surely called me from below the sheet. At the same time, though, I thought I heard a door squeaking downstairs; it was time to go. I didn't care about the telescope's lenses anymore, I had something much more interesting now.

So I quietly retraced my steps back to the house and I carefully locked the attic's door. Passing by two doors of the emptied rooms, my room being the next, I thought it would be wise to leave the box on my bed before going back to the kitchen. And so I did, though not without a degree of effort; I didn't want to leave it behind, I didn't want to be separated from it. Walking down the stairs, when I was on the last step, I was shocked by the scene. Charlize was there, standing in the middle of the living room, frozen, staring at the front door. I quickly turned the flashlight off; I thought I would die. My heart was jumping out of my mouth, I couldn't even scream in terror; I barely could breathe. A few minutes had passed until I regained lucidity; she remained there, immobilized. And then it occurred to me that she could be a sleepwalker. I could never have imagined that; I never left my bed at night before, never went to sleep after her.

When I realized what was going on, I rapidly tiptoed to the kitchen and returned the keys to the key box, each one to its proper place in order not to raise suspicion. Coming back to the living room and walking up the stairs, and keeping a close eye on her, she stood there just as before. It was the scariest thing I've ever seen at the time. I went back to my room in less than one minute and promptly hid the box below my dresser; after which I jumped into my sheets. Soon I would have to get up for school. I couldn't fall asleep with ease though, I couldn't stop thinking about the box, imagining what treasures could be in there. And as I did so, I spoke in silence to my friends, the stars. I wished there was something inside the box that I could share with the stars. They were glimmering brighter than ever that night; I thought they were happy for me. Additionally, I was somehow relieved, for Charlize's recently discovered sleepwalking explained, in a way, the footsteps I often heard at night.

On the following morning, I felt exhausted. I didn't sleep a wink and I didn't want to go to school, but I had to. I couldn't help having a look inside the box before though. It was calling me, in a way that is hard to describe with words. It was a craving; it was like water inviting me when I am thirsty. And I was thirsty. When I opened it, I saw a curious locket, along with a notebook and a red leather book. My first reaction was to grab the pendant; it had an odd engraving, a symbol, surrounded by unusual inscriptions in an unknown alphabet. I opened it and inside it was engraved the sentence *"fais ce que voudras"* in circular form; I knew this was French, but I didn't know what it meant. I immediately put it around my neck, under my shirt, and proceeded to explore the other items.

The notebook had my mother's name on it: Lynette. I decided I would explore it later, to dedicate to it the attention it deserved. Lastly, the red leather book looked very old; I skimmed through it and realized it was also written in French, and had strange illustrations of word squares, number squares, Sun and Moon motifs, and symbols I recognized from the book on Astronomy I was allowed to read. I guess the title was "Dogme et Rituel de l'Enfant de la Lune" and the author was Jacques Deshayes; I'm not sure I'm spelling it correctly. All seemed extraordinarily interesting, but I had to go. I heard Charlize walking up the stairs; I was late. I quickly closed the box and returned it to its former place, under the dresser. It would be safe there. This, however, required an extreme effort and great determination, for the box seemed not to want to let me go.

At school, three of the boys who often bullied me came to make fun of me and beat me. They didn't need a reason, it was always like that. One of them called me weirdo, the other, a freak. I asked them to stop, I asked them why they did this to me, to which one of them—whom behaved like the leader—said, "because you are an abortion, the son of a vampire". At this moment, the school bell rang and they made a dash for class. I stood there on my knees staring in anger while they ran. Suddenly, the locket on my neck became hotter and hotter, I felt like it was burning my skin. That was when I saw the leader of the bullies fall on the stairs and break his teeth. "Well done!" I thought, but at the same time my self-satisfaction in witnessing his humiliation was mixed with fright, for I knew the pendant somehow did it. It became metal cold again as soon as the boy fell. I knew there was a connection.

Coming back home that afternoon, I delved into my mother's diary. In the first pages, most of the entries were concerned with her recently-discovered disease by the end of the seventies, possibly derived from an infertility treatment. They spoke of her frustrations and her immense desire to be a mother, of her lack of faith. There was also an entry about the funeral of Charlize's husband, and my mother's intention in asking permission to my father and invite her to live with them. In the beginning of the eighties, according to the dates recorded in the diary, things started to become really weird. One entry went like:

June 23RD, 1984

I saw Dr. Campbell today. He said our chances to have a child are increasing. Howie says he doesn't trust him and blames the treatment for my condition. He has completely lost faith in medicine. He is very enthusiastic, on the other hand, about his activities in the Textile Club. He said he is learning a mystical operation from the guys there. He calls it "Qulielfi Operation"; sometimes he refers to it as "Moonchild Procedure" instead. He is totally convinced that this is the best option for us, and that it will certainly work. But according to him, we have to wait until the stars are right.

Another entry spoke of which stars more clearly.

December 27TH, 1984

Howie said that the stars will be right tonight; it is time for the "Qulielfi Operation". It has something to do with the Moon in conjunction with the Pleiades at mid-heaven. He is now busy preparing our room with candles and strange symbols drawn with chalk. I am afraid. I desperately want this child, but I fear we lose our souls in this pagan intercourse. He said he will summon an entity he calls "The Marquis" while we make love, so the entity will open a tunnel to another dimension, from which one of the denizens, craving to be born, will miraculously fix my infertility. It gives me the creeps just thinking about it. I am both excited and frightened; I hope our dear Lord forgives us for this.

So this perhaps explained why my father was such a night sky aficionado; I guess he became obsessed with the time the stars would be right. I spent the whole afternoon reading the diary and noticed several pages were missing. It looked like my parents were preparing for some kind of ritual. My mother didn't seem to fully agree, but from what I could understand from her words, my father forced her. As tired as I was, I almost fell asleep on the diary.

I thought it would be better return it to the box below the dresser and leave it to be explored on the following day.

At dinner, Charlize was in a bad mood as usual, but she was slightly different; I didn't know what it was. Upon my slurping, she overreacted by punching the table. "Why does it have to be always like this? When are you going to set me free? You little beast! Dinner is over. Go to your room." There was something different with her eyes. I was terrified. I quickly went up to brush my teeth and made my way to bed. I was so tired I didn't have trouble sleeping. However, I had a terrible nightmare that night, worse than any I've ever had; so vivid.

I dreamed my mother (I assumed it was my mother) was lying on a wake table, dressed in a white nightdress, surrounded by candles, in a dark and suffocating chamber. All of a sudden she got up and looked at me; her face was pale, her eyes were blank and there was no spark in them. In a flat voice, she begged me to give her my blood, for she was thirsty. She seemed hypnotized and her movements were somewhat mechanical, as if controlled by a non-human operator. I felt ice on my spine; my terror was such that I woke up. But, to my distress, I remained paralysed. I was unable to move any part of my body except my eyes. At the foot of the bed, an abhorrent, huge black figure was staring at me with its red eyes; they shined like the stars. I tried to shout, but I couldn't, all that came out was a muffled "mmmm". I barely could breathe. I don't know how long it lasted, this state of paralysis, but it appeared to be an eternity. But as soon as the creature disappeared, I was able to move again. I was shocked, this never happened before.

On the following morning, Mr. Gagnon came to care for the garden; it was Saturday. I didn't mention anything of the terrible experiences I was having, neither about the box nor the locket. I asked him, though, how could I learn French. He had no idea. "Try a dictionary," he said, "the school library must have one". I thought it was a good idea. But I would have to wait until Monday. I stood there, watching him care for the flowers until lunchtime. He asked me if something happened to Charlize that would explain her different countenance. He also noticed. I replied that I didn't know, that it must be related to the death anniversary of her husband; who knows?

In the afternoon, I went back to my room and decided to explore the red book. Even without a dictionary, I might be able to discover something. The book was amazing, gorgeous! And also macabre. I caught myself hypnotized, more than once, by its illustrations and typography. It had a strange influence on my feelings. I flipped through the book like this for hours, I didn't even see the evening coming. I saw the word "Qulielfi"—exactly like that—in my mother's diary, more than twice in its pages, as much as the word Pleiades, written "Pléiades". I also recognized an extract of a star chart in one of the pages, focusing on seven stars and surrounded by strange characters composed by lines and circles. At the bottom of the drawing, there was also an unfamiliar seal that looked like a signature. I quickly looked at the window wondering if I could find those stars in the night sky.

I automatically left the book aside on the bed and ran to the window, fantasizing about the stars. It was just for a moment, but it was enough to allow Charlize to enter the room unnoticed. When I turned around, I shivered when I saw her; she was staring at me and then moved her eyes to the foot of the bed, to the book. She approached it very calmly and took it in her hands, wide-eyed. She didn't say a word, but as she flipped through the book her expression became heavier and heavier. After a while, she left my bedroom in a rush, as if reaching for something, taking the book with her. Then, in less than a minute she reappeared with her wooden ruler and came in my direction, aiming to beat me.

However, as soon as she lifted her hand, her arm became paralyzed in the air, as if someone was holding it from behind. She became confused, frightened, and even more infuriated. From the corner of my eye, I saw the abhorrent creature with red eyes that watched me, holding her arm. My pendant again became hotter and hotter; the more she fought to release herself, the hotter the pendant became and the worse she had gotten entangled. I asked the creature to stop and let her go, but it wouldn't listen. "Live her alone, Marquis!" I shouted; then it finally let her go and vanished in the air. A sudden headache took over me, and having not been satisfied, Charlize came again on my direction and aimed for my neck. She tried to strangle me. But then, the creature appeared once more and, with a single blow, threw her out of my bedroom and over the hand railing directly to the living room's floor, not without first hitting a three-armed candle holder.

I ran to the stairs to find her insentient body stretched on the floor, surrounded by the flames on the carpet that was already afire. Horrified, I took off the necklace and threw it away. The headache grew stronger and stronger to the point that I passed out. The only thing I recall after this is that I was outside, in front of the house and under the rain, with the flashing lights of the police cars. I don't remember very well, but it appears I was in shock, staring at the house being burned down. Charlize was not found alive. She was the worst aunt ever but she was my only family. Now I was alone. Mr. Gagnon came as soon as he could, after being informed by a neighbour who also called the police. It was relieving to see a familiar face amid all that chaos. I was devastated, catatonic.

The causes of the fire were investigated and the report of the investigation was inconclusive. The cops obviously didn't believe my story and they couldn't find the locket or my mother's diary, nor the red book, which could have corroborated at least part of my testimony. According to them, the most probable cause was that an intruder broke in the house and the theft might have gone wrong at one point, so the home invader pushed Charlize down the stairs and the house was accidentally set on fire during the confusion. They thought the black figure with red eyes of my version referred to the intruder, that quite possibly it was the way a thirteen-year-old child would have dealt with such a stressful situation.

The local press, however, threw the suspicion that I pushed Charlize down the stairs and set the house on fire, a suspicion that was not corroborated by the police. The headlines mentioned "The Monster of Concord", referring to me, and also mocked my story of the black figure with red eyes. Charlize, or what was left of her, was buried at Old North Cemetery, in my father's family tomb. I, on the other hand, was transferred to an orphanage, wherein my nightmares became worse and the sleep paralysis more frequent. My horrible guardian accompanied me and I often saw it from the corner of my eye for a long time, before the pills. Mr. Gagnon kindly visited me in the orphanage, every fifteen days; he was the only that showed compassion and seemed to believe me. "Your father might have meddled with unadvisable unknown forces", he said.

My obsession and nightmares grew so strong as I became older that they transferred me to the New Hampshire Hospital to receive mental care. And here I live since the end of the 90's. Mr. Gagnon always managed to come and visit me, and when he was too old to come, he started sending his son instead; Elliot, the father of the deceased little girl. He also believes my story. Elliot has been helping me to study the occult and the supernatural and try to understand what kind of creature and experience was that. All conducted in secrecy, though, for the doctors asked him not to stimulate thoughts of the tragedy. Mr. Gagnon unfortunately passed away recently and on the day after the funeral, Elliot brought me your book, in which I saw many similarities with Jacques Deshayes' red book. Elliot never found an author by the name Jacques Deshayes or any book with "l'Enfant de la Lune" in the title. But we believe "The Marquis" may be one of the spirits in your book. Please, I need your help; I need you to show them I am not crazy and that these things really exist. Will you talk to the hospital? Please.

Yours truly,
David Juilliard

This was a letter I received through my Publisher by the end of 2013. Perplexed, I did not know how to answer and, therefore, never did. I hope David is well and has managed to recover from his trauma. Some things are better left as they are.

A DRESS OF EGGSHELL BLUE

by Paul F. Newman

No one lived at 134 East Street anymore. It was just an empty place in an American town; drab, north facing, sunless. Folks crossed the cinder track to pass on the other side and most avoided looking. Were there down-and-outs living in the dark of the old mansion? No one cared to find out. Front steps led to a recessed door that led to a lobby skulking in shadow. People steered clear. "It didn't used to be like that," the grown-ups would say.

The kids said it was haunted. Any empty old building was plainly full of cobwebs, coffins and ghosts, you know what kids are like, but one thing did scare me. There was talk of a witch who haunted the lobby. Maybe it was a story put around to keep trespassers out, but it worried me because once or twice when I was small, I'd seen a beautiful lady standing at the entrance, and I'd never seen her anywhere else. The lady was certainly not a witch; she stood in the breeze with her sun hat and her golden hair that hung to her shoulders, and the dress she wore was so delicate and blue it reminded me of forget-me-nots and bird's eggs. I'd heard older people speak in hushed tones of a lady called Felicity Lee and I used to think it was her. But it couldn't have been because she was dead.

It happened back in the war years when the able-bodied men were serving our country far away and returned only briefly on leave, if return they did. My father was one, he was in the Navy, and though I was born in forty-three I didn't know him proper till the war ended. Meantime if a job needed doing back in our neigh-bourhood it fell to the same motley gang of old-timers, pimply youths, and shifty-eyed objectors to get it done.

"The Dirty Dozen" folks called them. A loose round-up of masculinity ranging from weathered craftsmen like Jim and Jake Rogers to intellectual red-eyes like Daniel Fremont, grinning ado-lescents like Toady Malone, and alcoholic bums like Amos Harris. New building construction was unusual at that time; most work was of a repairing nature, just fixing things to make do, but before the war a new shopping parade had been planned on East Street and the scaffolding erected. This two-storey site of market stores would be directly opposite the haunted house—although in those days 134 East Street was a proud and sunny building, very much alive. The Mayor agreed that work on the new parade should con-tinue despite the war and The Dirty Dozen laboured at it in a leis-urely fashion between other business. If anyone wanted a leaky pipe fixed or a broken fence repaired they knew where to go to find the boys—down on East Street.

Felicity Lee was a young woman who lived in the grand old block on East Street and whenever she walked out or stood on the front steps the guys over the road would lay down their tools, whistle and call and all but fall off their perches. Felicity pretended not to hear but she came out more and more and stood on the steps dressed like she was going to a ball or on her way to a picnic with a movie star.

To cut the story short, Felicity succumbed to the attractions of one of the fellows, one of The Dirty Dozen. People said it was Dan Fremont but no one talks of it much. Dan was a handsome man, mid-twenties I guess, with a clever way of talking by all accounts. He belonged to some unusual religion that didn't allow violence so he was exempted from the military call-up and the regular church-going folks didn't like him much because of that. Anyway, he fell in the river and drowned soon after. It kind of shut people up who had been bad-mouthing him and nobody wanted to say much more about it.

Dan and Felicity had started seeing each other, meeting somewhere private, but she still looked for him over the road when she came out on the front steps in the light of day. If he was there, she would smile, lower her eyes and move on. If he wasn't she would act as if she never looked.

Then one day she came out looking kind of anxious. It seemed she was searching for Dan like she had something to tell him, the other fellows said. And Dan was more animated than usual and came down to the roadside and waved and called across, and she ran without looking and went straight under the wheels of a delivery truck.

It was a dreadful accident. Right in front of all the boys and only a yard or so in front of Dan. She died outright. The delivery driver was from out of town and he was so shook up he never drove a truck again. Someone had to come in special and take him home. Dan blamed himself too, they reckon. He didn't come to her funeral. He had drowned the day before.

In the months that followed the men carried on with their building but the atmosphere had changed. No more skylarking and pranking, no more free and easy invitations to "Come and find me down on East Street". Now it was quiet and serious. They wanted the job over. They wanted to get away. So the building was finished sooner than expected: the store fronts, the upstairs apartments; properly built, mind you, and after the war new owners occupied them and made them light and cheerful. But the new building's height cast a permanent shade over the opposite side of the street. The front steps where Felicity once stood in the sun were shrouded in gloom. One by one the occupants of the old mansion moved on to newer and brighter homes in other parts of town.

And that was it. Although it was a sad story, for many years I treasured those glimpses of the blue lady. The lady who was killed about the same time as I was born I guess. Somehow I could never convince myself she was a ghost; the feeling was too warm, too— how shall I put it—*modern*. It didn't feel like something dead and gone. If anything I wished that some day I could grow up to be like her. Then the years passed and I moved with my parents to a different city with busy streets and bustling traffic and big schools with teenage friends and I grew up fast and my country childhood seemed a thousand years behind.

*

Now it's 1961. I am eighteen and a proper lady. I work at *Hayes*, a large retail store on the high street that pays well but I'm continuing my education at night school. I've grown very interested in psychology and paranormal experiences, I read about things like that all the time. I think I have a gift that way. *Meet the Inner Child* is a fabulous book I'm reading right now that describes techniques for travelling back and meeting yourself just as you were when you were very small. I'm trying hard to master it.

My other great love, apart from boys of course, is clothes and fashion. I guess I have always been interested, right back to when I saw the beautiful lady on East Street and wanted to look like her. Guess what! This summer I bought a really sophisticated wide-brimmed sun hat, just like hers, and I have a light floaty summer dress of eggshell blue that could have been the very one she wore. It's a little revealing, but I don't care. I feel strong and confident dressed that way. I wear my hair at shoulder length too. It's light auburn just like the beautiful lady's.

Important things always seem to happen when I wear this dress. Only last week, I couldn't believe it, I was working behind my desk at the store when who should come over but Toady Malone! He must be all of thirty now and really not bad looking at all. I recognized him straightaway and after a moment he remembered me and we fell to chatting fit to burst. I saw the supervisor craning her neck, so we agreed to meet again in my lunch hour. Toady—I didn't call him that, I learnt his real name was Philip—insisted on buying me a Peach Melba in a really expensive ice-cream parlor. It was gorgeously soft and cold and juicy, and as I stirred the long spoon in the glass I said it was like amber nectar, and he said it was like the colour of my hair. I thought perhaps he might remark that

I looked like Felicity Lee, for I was wearing that blue dress, but he didn't, and after we'd talked of what we had both done in the years since I left the old town, I cautiously raised the subject again.

"Do you remember her?" I asked.

"Sure do," his eyes looked far away, "She always looked so stunning. It wasn't just her raven black hair but the tight red dresses she used to wear. She always wore red. It must have been her favorite color. They reckon she was pregnant. That's what she was trying to tell Dan Fremont when she… ran across the street."

My world turned a cartwheel. Felicity Lee wore red? Felicity Lee had black hair? This wasn't the Felicity I knew, or thought I knew. Philip was describing someone quite different. In a shattering moment I realized I had nothing to do with the unlucky Felicity. Her story was nothing more to me than a warning not to lose one's head where men were concerned. So who was the other lady, the lovely blue lady I had seen in that same place and that I believed I had become?

My God it was me. It was really me. It surely means that any day this summer when I'm wearing this dress I will return and meet myself as a child. I will have mastered the technique. This knowledge alone boosted my confidence to try the exercise in earnest as soon as I got home. And I would meet myself at 134 East Street because that was imprinted with such heavy emotion and it connected me to Philip who brought me the revelation of who I am.

THE NECRONOMICON, SUMERIAN HISTORY, AND THE ANTIQUITY BEHIND IT

by Suzanne Divinsky

This is Ningishzidda speaking. I am an entity of extraterrestrial origins, yet born on planet Earth. I personally decided to come forth on this subject as I consider it of great importance in this epic time of history. My roots are of the Anunnaki race from planet Nibiru, sometimes called the twelfth planet in the Solar System, a passerby of approximately every 3,600 years. I have dwelled on this planet for more than three hundred thousand years. There is a lot I could say about scads of things, however I will limit my comments to certain parts of the manuscripts in *The Necronomicon,* according to the writings of the so-called Mad Arab (the "Mad Arab" is an anagram for a man with a direct genetic bloodline of my old scribe, Madar Abdhul Alhazred). However, the varieties of the Necronomicon manuscripts available today are not identical to the original, since the variances of both John Dee and H.P. Lovecraft's versions are craftily and deliberately riffed by the Arab (as I prefer to call him, since he was in no way mad or mentally retarded, he just did not entirely realize what he was actually dealing with: the truth about human origins, extra-terrestrial beings transformed into atrocious demons). Furthermore, he put different versions in all five of the originals, which are meant to be read one after the other in a specific order.

Let me go on with explaining my name, Ningishzidda. My mother Ereshkigal gave it to me, and my father Enki consented. It metaphorically means "Lord of the Illuminated Tree". I have been given many monikers, among them Trismegistus, Quetzalcoatl, Tehuti, as well as Thoth, and A'an. My primary label has three meanings: the first referring to the Tree of Wisdom, as concerning the spirals—or serpents—of the three dimensional helix lingering inside human DNA; the second denoting an old cosmic artifact connected to the Flower of Life; and the third signifying the Tree of Knowledge, a construction that can exclusively be illuminated by the Wise. I have foreseen the time of the Dragon to reemerge and this is the incarnation, as the Great Dragon returned in 2012; all according to the impressive prophecy kept by the Wise, the Savants of the Ages, the old souls that have incarnated in this important time. In other words, the rendezvous of Past and Future and the return of the Ancients.

Furthermore I wish to offer you five significant actualities:

1. You can call on us, summon us if you like, but we are not demons, neither gods, nor humans. As I said, we are of a different kind, not distant from yours. My name is related to the origins of humankind as I was part of the trinity that once created the human race, approximately three hundred thousand years ago. Names and titles are important, as they in one way predict an individual's fate and future, and at the same time connect to the past and present. When a person's name is compelled into a seal it becomes even more commanding, whether this individual is of demonic nature or not.

2. In the Necronomicon a lot of names and titles are collected, all of them individuals of the Nibirian race, the Anunnaki if you prefer. I will let you in on my ancestor tree, starting with Anu, previous king of planet Nibiru, the home of our breed. Anu was my grandfather, Enki is my father, and Enlil my uncle. They constitute the trinity which in the Necronomicon is called "The

Elders". Marduk is my half-brother, Ereshkigal was my mother, Inanna my aunt, and Nannar/Sin my grandfather. I could go on bothering you with my genetic lineage to no avail but for showing you a different point of view according to these texts; a veracity that has been hidden for an extended period, wrapped up by calling us demons and whirling the whole thing into an occult framework. Demons are real all right, but they exist in different dimensions from where we normally and psychically interact, and even if humans and Nibirians are of different breeds, we are of the same mettle.

3. I personally have different names and titles in diverse cultures, some of them as follows: Tehuti, Thoth, Quetzalcoatl, Kukulkan, Kulla, Hermes, Mercury, Itza, and Trismegistus. The same goes for my relatives, as well as the factual gods, which to us were the celestial divinities, a.k.a. planets and stars. The most mixed title is the one of Marduk, the entity with fifty names, as Marduk was also another designation for the planet Nibiru. In the beginning, before we propertied the Earth, we called Earth the blue planet, the seventh planet, or Ki (as Ki is the remainder of a previous and much larger planet called Tiamat, or The Dragon). In the beginning, as in the creation stories told by the Nibirian sages—the Royal Savants, that also, and to my enjoyment, can be read about in the Necronomicon—a Moon of Nibiru/Marduk crashed into Tiamat/The Dragon and split her into two separate fragments. One part is the planet now called Earth, and the other piece was smashed into fragments and sent out to form the asteroid belt, or the Hammered Belt, as we call it. Kingu was the satellite of Tiamat that remained with Ki/Earth and became its moon. We can read in the Necronomicon that the human race was created from the blood of the Moon. I do not know where the Arab got this fabrication from, to me it seems like a misinterpretation from the other myth which embraces that the first humans were made from clay (which is also a veracity with alteration, and off topic in this case, but nevertheless of importance and to be further de-

veloped in other texts).

4. While reading the Necronomicon you realize that the names of my relatives are also the names of planets, as we shared titles with the celestial bodies in the sky, which were somewhat our gods, as they reside in the heavens. This is the ancient history of how the Solar System was fashioned by the Creator of All. These writings also concern the very foundations of the universe, and when Nibiru for the first time entered the order of Apsu (the Sun of the Earth). The symbol of the five-pointed star is, as the Arab correctly tells us, the depiction of the Arian race of Nibiru, as is the double-headed eagle, which is also the insignia of my cousin Ninurta. The fleur-de-lis is the representation of the descendants of Lord Anu, former King of Nibiru.

5. Concerning the Qliphoth, I manufactured the innovative versions together with my cousin Ninurta (in the Necronomicon labeled "Ninib"). Ninurta was also the tutor of Cain, as Cain was expelled from Mesopotamia to South America. My father Enki commenced The Brotherhood of the Snake, an instruction that later became the foundation of the Kabbalah, even though they missed sequences that were of great importance—like the lessons of the Moon, the left hand path, the negative, the black polarity of the Sun, the dark bright light, and the true Malkhut —or the occult, as you would say, but it only became occult as this form of knowledge was hidden and repressed. I personally exceeded all expectations mastering this worthwhile education, but I kept the secret teachings away from those who did not want humankind to be educated. In some ways you can say that the Qliphothic knowledge is connected to the wisdom of Sophia, brought from womanhood, the original womb, through the Nibirian race and further on to the mankind of today, Homo sapiens sapiens. Unfortunately, the Homo sapiens idaltu were extinct.

Addendum:

Ninurta educated the descendants of Cain (who killed his twin brother, however not on purpose, as he did not yet know about death). The father of Abel and Cain was a great adept of my tutoring, he lived for ninety thousand years and was a half blood of the lineage of my father, begotten with a female hybrid, also genetically engineered. Cain passed on the traditions of masonry and blacksmithing—which Ninurta imparted to him—to his offspring. In the days of Tubal-Cain, some of Cain's descendants were brought to Egypt and became Pharaohs. One of them was Akhenaten. His elongated skull was a genetic resolution made by myself on command of my father, Enki, the Father of All (so titled as his semen, during the ages, was spread over the continents).

It was ultimately after my uncle Enlil distorted my father's work in The Brotherhood of the Snake that I instigated The Order of the Black Serpent and kept the knowledge hidden, secret, or as you might say, occult. Unfortunately, this directed all sorts of confusion and misapprehensions. Sealing the Qliphot with demons was on the one hand the smartest design in history, on the other hand it was a total mishap. Working with the Great Dragon is the most innocuous way to convey this sovereign knowledge, as in the teachings of the reformed Order of the Serpent. I entirely give recognition to the way this is carried on by the Order of the Dragon, and I am prepared to fill in any absent fragments. I will be your utmost and unassuming servant in a selfsame inverted way. This will be my gift to the esoteric and magical sciences of the contemporary world, if we prefer to perceive it as such (at least it is fashionable in the overhaul of current terms). Having memories of virtually three hundred thousand years is not always as decent as it appears, when it carries with it a ration of responsibilities. I need to have clemency for what has occurred along the way and of what has been left out from the teachings of the ancient times. I sense the wings of the Red Dragon closer than yet before, and recognize it will exult with the Black Serpent, or whatever insignia the aforementioned might have.

Finally, I will make it known that Atlantis was somewhat an island situated between the two rivers of Mesopotamia, Euphrates and Tigris. Lemuria on the other hand was a space station we organized on planet Mars ("Lehmu" in our language) from where the non-royal laborers of Nibiru went down and seized for themselves the daughters of men. Mu was the olden space center on Nibiru whither the gold from Earth was sent …

Ponder not why Magus Crowley wrote his own Necronomicon in the shadow of The Great Pyramid of Giza in old Khem, as I was the explicit architect of the building.

In the name of Ningishzidda, Pentamegistus, Lord of the Illuminated Tree.

TOMB OF LILITH

By Isfet

As I wandered through life dissatisfied,
Having felt an otherworldly longing since birth,
I came upon an old crypt door, mystified,
And with hopes of extinguishing my existential dearth
Down, down I went into the putrid earth.
Deep down inside that catacomb,
I found a world of wondrous extremes,
Where dark beings of origins unknown,
Weave a web of dark dreams,
And in the distance, the transcendent gleams.
Fear and desire ran through me unbound, Joy, terror,
lust, mad acts of devilry, Enchanting phantasmagoria
profound, Otherworldly dreams revealed resplendently,
I embraced it all in ecstasy.
My mind and spirit profoundly changed,
As I reemerged from that bizarre womb,
I looked upon the mundane world, now strange,
The blessing and curse of having been exhumed,
Reborn anew, from a tomb!

FATAL FORMULAES

By Sjunde Inseglet

in the fouled substance of god, in the violence of quietude
in an hour most austere, we alter the web of fate
azag galra sabi mu unna te!
may your joy be as festive as a million droughts
namtar galra zibi mu unna te!
may your love be as pristine as rotten wine
utuk zul gubi mu unna te!
may your hope be as vivid as mummified flesh
ala xul gabi mu unna te!
may the doors stay forever locked
and the bare walls lead you into madness
we will not forgive, nor will we forget
when hungering you'll be given soil to eat
when thirsting you'll be given oil to drink
we will not forgive, nor will we forget
Azag galra sagbi mu unna te!
Namtar galra zibi mu unna te!
Utuk xul gubi mu unna te!
Ala xul gabi mu unna te!
Gidim xul ibbi mu unna te!

(dedicated to "A")

RITE DE PASSAGE

by Julien Bert

The cold and moist sand, under my bare feet, gave an impression that I was treading the ground of an old chapel that was abandoned for centuries and upon which a fatal curse seemed to weigh; chills were going right through my whole body, as though the serpent was about to arise. It was pitch dark. It was one of those starless winter nights when only the beams of a scarlet moon could tear the darkness of the sky and when the piercing whistles of a few nighthawks seemed to herald any macabre tragedy. The ocean was seemingly calm and serene, strangely contrasting with my immediate surroundings.

The presence of humans was not so remote from the place —after all, the closest homes were located just a few dozen miles from this beach on the Atlantic coast, not far from the town of Arkham. Nevertheless, accessing this place, which was only possible by walking along high and steep cliffs through a very narrow trail, proved to be particularly difficult and even dangerous—and, in fact, it had been the site of tragic accidents in the past—with the result that the place, considered evil by the least audacious and the most superstitious people, was very little frequented, and obviously even less by night. But that night, perhaps more than ever, every trace of life—except for mine—seemed to have abandoned this spot that was surrounded by the elements. I was standing, in the nude, looking out into the horizon, this demarcation line between sky and ocean. Waiting for Her "signal"...

For how long had I been there? Some hours? Several weeks? A couple of years? An eternity? I was literally unable to answer the question, and to tell the truth, it didn't matter any longer. It even seemed that I had lost all spatio-temporal reference points. What I was looking for since time immemorial—without even knowing it—and that upon which I had been focusing all my efforts was finally within reach. After fixing my gaze in this sumptuously tragic landscape I had penetrated this famous "crack" within reality, this gate to the Other Side that a few ones only are able to glimpse in the middle of a piece of classical music or at the bend of a forest trail. I had been able—at least temporarily—to free myself from the shackles of the frightful Hindu goddess, the mother of time and illusion who makes man a mere pawn moving slowly and with no actual goal on the chessboard which one believes to be one's very own existence... And upon which one thinks that one can get some grip... You poor thing!

The memories of the last days' events—and notably this particular dream in which She had undeniably played a prominent role—were tumbling in my mind, with no logic nor chronology, forcing me, as if I were a cryptologist, to follow a breadcrumb trail and then bring together the pieces of this occult puzzle, with the final goal of unraveling its hidden meaning. Then everything became subtly clear. How could I have missed what was obvious, without even envisioning it? It is sometimes necessary to close one's eyes in order to see the invisible...

Suddenly, in the silence of death, I was awakened from this state of torpor by a dreadful—or demonic should I say—howling. Had this been the cry of an injured animal? I was unable to say. But I had never heard such a sound in my whole life and, according to me, it could not have emanated from anything belonging to our world. My eyes, now accustomed to the dark, spontaneously headed for the position where I thought the scream originated from, but they could not identify anything nor even distinguish anything unusual. In any event, I was, suddenly and against my will, brought back to the reality of this winter night. This turned my blood cold—was it fear or rather some kind of intense exaltation?—and my psyche, suddenly inundated by antinomian feelings, refused, as if to protect itself from a mortal danger, to recognize what seemed evident though: the time was finally now.

Following my instinct – or perhaps my reptilian brain – I ran from the beach and instantly plunged into the icy waves. The water temperature was clearly not much above 40°F, and I felt there were thousands of tiny tongues of cold steel burning all the surface of my skin. But that was just an insignificant detail. At that point it seemed to me that nothing could thwart my plans any longer. Although my limbs were numb due to the coldness I was now swimming with determination towards the open water, struggling against the sea which actually proved much rougher than it had appeared to me from the shore, a little earlier. Unless the weather had suddenly decided to unleash its wrath, as if prompted by Lil's invisible force...

In a fraction of a second, as if I was trying to turn back and remove myself from a situation that could have led to my loss, I took a brief look towards the beach, but I had once again lost all visual reference and, as of now, did find myself in the middle of the ocean which had always been a source of fascination for me, though sometimes viewed with apprehension and circumspection. It was at that time that I lost control over my willpower—or at least what was remaining of it —like a sailor captivated by the sultry voice of any sea creature, and that I ended up being pulled below the surface, to the ocean's depths, as under direct influence of a tentacle or serpentine entity which would have coiled around my legs and hips. At the thought of ending up drowned or imagining that my body could serve as food to the ocean's most voracious fish, an anguish of death suddenly overwhelmed me. However, contrary to all expectations, I realized that the strictly physical constraints—such as the need to bring air to my lungs—had simply disappeared; from now on I was wholly belonging to the realm of Poseidon, I had the feeling of being totally at ease with the mercurial element, the world's generating principle.

At this point was I the unconscious victim of dreamlike visions, or had insanity invaded the whole space of my psyche? I didn't know. Just like a heavy key made of steel—in search of any door to unlock—I surrendered and let myself be irremediably dragged to the coldness and dark of the bottomless Abyss, determined to abandon a part of myself there and in the hopes of discovering the treasure of some ancient civilization that would be hidden there for millennia. As I was sinking, I got rid of all fear, and feelings of serenity and "letting go" slowly invaded my being. I was remembering Az(ath)oth's wise and ageless teachings according to which it is only after sincerely confronting one's own darkness that true light spurts in man.

The sun was beginning to rise above the horizon, thereby making New England's skies—which until then had bathed in darkness—go purple. The waves had resumed their smooth and regular movement, and started to slowly cover the beach with their transparent and sparkling shroud. All evidence of the ritual which had held there a few hours ago would soon disappear forever to inexperienced eyes. The sigil, drawn in the sand by the magician, had already lost its splendor. The womb's harmonious curves, that da Vinci could have described as a stylized— or qliphotic—picture of the Grail, were irremediably disappearing under the repeated assault of these graceful but tireless waves. A back and forth which meant that life was incrementally blossoming again, that order was going to follow chaos, once more. An expression of satisfaction came upon the face of Babylon's solar sovereign; he had just laid the Primordial Goddess low, leaving her sink again into a restful and deserved slumber. However, according to the immemorial cosmic laws, a new confrontation would soon occur and reverse the order of things...

STEP TO THE OTHER SIDE

By Victor Hernandez

It was nine o'clock at night. Thom was illuminating the figure of a little fairy that his mother had given him at his request. He paused a moment and put a little silver glow, because the fairy was magical, he said, and for that reason it should shine. The lamp that was above his head radiated its light softly. Thom's imagination was so great that the fairy's wings shone brightly, projecting its sparkles into his deepest imagination. In an instant, he saw the beating of its wings just like a hummingbird, it seemed that the fairy was freed from the sheet of paper to fly throughout the room. Thom heard clearly how the fairy whispered words that he could not understand, as if they belonged to an ancient language. The words were so elegant but they scared him.

An aura emanated from the fairy's body, which intensified when she ascended. Thom looked at her in amazement, she was so beautiful. Slowly the fairy ascended and a cold wind ran through Thom's legs that passed up his back until it reached his head. Then, kaleidoscopic flashes blinded him, transporting him to what looked like a tunnel; his heart was pounding a thousand beats an hour, the sweat on his forehead fell and his hands tingled without him knowing why.

Suddenly in the distance, what looked like a kind of portal manifested itself, was an iron door that slowly opened. Among a combination of fear and joy, Thom was attracted by a gravitational force that yielded to his resistance. But something inside him longed to enter that strange and gloomy place. The reality of his room distorted, the strange language whispered by the fairy was so clear that he seemed to understand it! "Hail, Hail, Hail". Thom wondered what that meant. Suddenly he found himself at the threshold of that gate and an aroma similar to incense was present, leaving his heart to pound and his hands to sweat. He heard the singing of some birds that reassured him, which later became whispers of female voices that were not fully understood.

As he crossed that threshold he looked everywhere, and immediately a winding road with golden veins was revealed before his eyes; these were on the walls of the tunnel making a mosaic of bright lights that guided his way. He wanted to touch them and take one of them, but they were out of reach. Only the road was at his disposal. He chose to follow the path laid before his eyes. When walking, it seemed that there was no time or space. The stress had passed, now he just felt peace and comfort. The image was opened across the road to show a green valley with chiaroscuros; as he walked, that brushstroke image blurred to become something more dreamlike.

He focused his gaze on the valley and noticed that there was a lake with a tree in the center, and in front of him, something bright was moving. Once again he heard "Hail, Hail, Hail." Thom approached, frowned, and with an insightful look, looked at a beautiful woman with a cape that fluttered in the wind.

He studied her carefully while she levitated a feather in the wind; that female figure was staring at him, he petrified himself with that radiant look and he wondered, "Is she the fairy?" The female held in her left hand a luminous crystal that seemed to have the shape of a snowflake; she extended her hand in offering and the glass was painted blue and white. Thom froze while waiting for something to happen. Suddenly, a violent ray traveled like a snake across the lake to hit him in the chest and leave him breathless.

But he did not fall, he only felt a force that flowed from the root of his spine and climbed up his back to explode in his head.

He shouted dreadfully, for he felt that his head would be about to break into a thousand pieces, but it was not so. His ears were deafened with a buzz; "Hail, Hail, Hail" repeated and two monstrous snakes zigzagged behind that woman, their movement reflected in Thom's dilated pupils.

The snakes were spiraling over each other to merge with the beautiful woman. A look of fire and a forked tongue were visible in that beautiful woman, white and slender; from it emerged silver wings and from its chest a crystal in the form of a bluish snowflake. That beautiful angel flew towards him to leave, but not before delivering to Thom the crystal. Thom took it in his hands and the glass gradually disintegrated to become a whitish vapor that he breathed in its entirety, permeating his interior with that essence that would transform him.

That being between angel and devil slowly moved away from Thom as a blurry image that accentuated as he stood in front of the tree, which was projected as a connection between heaven and earth. Now Thom was rising and a steed assisted him to take him away from the lake. He flew over the tree, but not before circling it to notice how beautiful and leafy it was; its interwoven branches branched from its roots to the same sky. The steed circled that tree, the demon/angel fused her female figure with the stoic trunk, her arms extended with the branches and finally her delicate hands with the green and pointed leaves.

Thom watched with a stony expression as the tree took on even more life, and from within he remembered when his grandfather one day told him that people at death were not received in any heaven or hell.

"Thom, every person, animal or thing has an energy deep inside, a divine spark that makes them who they are, and when death comes, the spirit separates from the physical body to merge into any tree that gives lodging; the tree that is in the back garden of the house is full of fruits and in it lives the spirit of your grandmother, that's why I take care of it so much."

As the tree came to life, the steed flew abruptly down into a vortex that violently sucked it in.

72

Thom was tense, face up with his eyes open. His eyeballs danced in the basins that contained them, a trismus prevented air from entering his mouth and his dilated pupils could no longer open. He was out of his consciousness. His mother entered the room and heard a creak and Thom saying strange things. She immediately assumed that a seizure had taken over him. Alarmed by the situation she took Thom by the neck and with a mother's care she gently grasped his head to make sure he was breathing. Suddenly Thom's gaze focused on his mother's face; he had regained consciousness.

Thom got up, confused, and did not remember anything. He sensed that something had happened; he did not feel the same, something inside him had changed but he could not define what. His worried mother told him that she would take him to the doctor because nothing like this had ever happened to him and she feared it was something serious.

Nine years later...

The tower looked like a mirage behind a veil of mist which emanated from the ground. Thom looked at his friend and said, "Did you bring the talisman with you?"

Paul nodded. At that moment Thom took a breath trying to fill his lungs. He supposed that this would give him momentum and more strength.

"I will walk to the next tree," and with his index finger he drew the path in the air.

Paul, with an insightful gaze focused on what appeared to be the entrance to the tower. In an instant, a roar was heard behind the mist, resonating beyond the cliffs covered by dense forest vegetation.

Air flowed in the forest. Thom's hands sweated and his pupils dilated to the fullest. A silhouette that was crawling in the shadows reflected in his pupils, and what appeared to be a torso was twisting and advancing. Paul then grasped the talisman hard, as if his life would depend on it. Fear was something that could end up destroying them, if they allowed it.

In the forest canopy a pale moon was hiding in the mist and a dozen logs stood as if they wanted to touch the night vault that the sky formed; the leaves clustered together, whispering in the cold wind that contracted their muscles. Paul and Thom looked at each other with narrowed eyes and the latter, with a gesture, asked his friend to approach.

There was a silence that only allowed for the creaking of the leaves to be heard at every step they gave. Suddenly, a moan of pain and despair was heard among the trees, covered with thick fog and terrifying darkness. Something in that night depth crawled slowly like a lizard to climb through a tree. Human-looking claws with hirsute skin, long fingernails and wet skin, clung to get the rest of the body to rise. That aberrant thing stood on two legs, about two meters long; and its eyes, like two obsidian sapphires, reflected the moonlight.

A beastly groan came out of his womb just to announce his presence and what appeared to be a pair of elongated and spastic legs held a rough abdomen and torso, where two fins that stood up to each excitement were inserted. Its willow curved enormously from side to side to show a devilish smile that showed dozens of sharp teeth like fine knives.

Paul fell back behind his friend, he placed one of his hands on Thom's right shoulder, poked his head over him and, as if in slow motion, a cold mist came out ahead of Thom's face. They both shuddered to see that the face of that horrifying creature showed a sardonic smile with a breath of fire. The devilish creature stared at them, their senses petrified; the mist caressed, like a mantle, every inch of his skin and it contracted...their minds clouded.

The tower looked so close and far at the same time. Paul, pointing, quick with his hand, "Look Thom!"

The creature was even more threatening when its upper limbs, like those of a large insect, showed remains of a dismembered body. A small breath of air behind their heads hedgehog the skin of both; they feared that their destiny was the same. It was time to take the talisman to the tower.

They ran without looking back, it was too late for regrets. The darkness gave no respite to two terrified young men fleeing. Tears of fear ran down Paul's cheeks, his agitated breathing contained the crying that was about to leave. In an instant, his voice became a scream when he felt behind him the elongated silhouette of that creature. The creature lifted him through the air with only one limb and, along with him, the talisman was lost in the tense darkness of the forest.

Thom didn't want to turn around, his own life was at stake. Paul fell with broken legs releasing a cry of pain that drowned him; his pupils dilated to the extreme, he groaned, clenched his teeth. He could no longer, his skin was torn. The screams of horror rumbled in Thom's head to the point of resonating in each of his bones; he vibrated until his stomach emptied into a bilious vomit. He hid behind a rock, peeked his head out and watched as his friend was dragged... into hell.

Silence and nothing else. He took a deep breath trying to contain the energy in his chest, he had to make his voice vibrate rhythmically, he knew what to say, it was just a matter of not losing his concentration because of fear, because that would kill him. He meditated; he knew that darkness possesses forces that can only be controlled with willpower. With his eyes closed he reached the required concentration until he modulated his heartbeat and with it his thoughts. He listened to his breath, inspired and exhaled.

From the depths of the forest came the echo of a roar that almost baffled Thom. He opened his mouth slightly and from it, words came out in the form of a mantra, with a rhythm that led him to an altered state of consciousness that calmed his mind and the wind. The silence of the forest was even more overwhelming than fear, the whisper of crowded leaves could not be heard. The mist opened to give way to the moonlight that fell on his head.

He opened his eyes; he was there. A dark figure without a face and anthropomorphic appearance inclined his head in greeting. The shadow moved towards the tower and halfway turned to Thom and with a gesture the dark figure invited him to follow him. Thom accelerated the passage and a few meters under his gaze to realize that just below his feet was the talisman, he reached out to take it off the ground, sat up and continued to continue on his way. Already at the threshold of the tower he stopped a moment to pull air, armed with courage and entered.

The walls of yesteryear flanked his path. He looked up and saw iron windows that were at a great distance, allowing with difficulty that a faint silver light seeped through. He had confidence within him, he had mastered fear; and with strength and security, he did not hesitate and walked towards the center of the tower. The dark being was already waiting for him, he reached out with his hand extended and Thom handed him the talisman. The infernal being approached him so closely that their faces almost touched. At that moment Thom looked at himself in the body of this being, and the shadow gave him a devilish smile that he returned.

The wind blew into the tower and a current flowed from the ground to drag its body from head to toe, subtly disintegrating into the clear night mist.

THE CROSSROADS AND THE HIDDEN FIEND

By Johannes K.

Not all crossroads are defined by the intersection of rural roads. Not all crossroads stir up that infamous image of Tommy Johnson signing a pact with the Devil in some accursed part of Mississippi. Some of them may appear at the most unlikely of places and the most unlikely of times. The crooked roads that take us to them are not always covered in dust. At times, you may find yourself walking downwards through the poisonous menstruum of some forgotten Goddess. At other times, a strange and numinous light may be flickering and calling you into a liminal plane of existence. You may even find yourself digging in grave soil until blood runs from underneath your fingernails, hungering for the forbidden knowledge of that which lurks below. What is true of crossroads, in the context given here, is that they represent beginnings rather than endings.

They are breaches and cracks that tear our conventions or general agreements of reality into pieces. They are thresholds to the Other side and constitute points where the strangest intrusions may occur. Within their reach the past, future, and present may be altered. In places like these, some divine poison flows in directions that causes us to question the precision of the web-like patterns constituting our intellects. Most have encountered such dire places in dreams and fantasies. Some may only know them from novels, stories, or the fantasies of others.

There are, however, ways and methods to initiate and spark such intrusions. I even daresay we may intrude the Other ourselves. Or, let me rephrase that: I know we can, but we will come to that at a later point. Certain ways of disrupting the fundaments of existence to such degrees that even the most stout-hearted soldier would sacrifice their life to avoid it have been passed down via cunning bloodlines for ages. An art that has endured many names and many forms still lives within our blood and lies dormant in the soil below us.

It has been passed down through the Goeten and the Hexes. Through madmen, despots, occultists, corrupted priests, and Diabolists. Such teachings lay within forgotten texts, sleeping until they are revived by those whose voices can reach into that which lies beyond. These teachings form a substratum of sinister fluid under the harsh wings of history. Not all of these teachers are human. Not all of them are hindered or limited by the ark of time. The fact of the matter is that the best teachers often are intruders themselves.

In the room where my first thoughts took form, there were seething horrors coming and going as if the doors to the Other were constantly ajar. In particular I experienced the intimate presence of an entity that simultaneously felt completely alien and as someone I had known for eternities. A distant, aching voice guarding me at night. With its horrors, another child was taking form within me as if growing in a womb at some stranger plane of existence. Following such events, I would find myself numb with horror. I would find myself staring right through the stranger in the mirror upon awakening the following day. I would begin to see an eerie gentleman wandering about in church as the priest held his weekly sermon. An odd glare would lure me to stray away from the school yard and withdraw to the strangest places, where games quite different from the ones I learned in school took place. This odd presence was initially somewhat ferocious and often filled me with both fear and curiosity. Over time, I would however find that each encounter stirred some emotive otherness. To provide some sort of didactic tool to the reader, we can call these phenomena numinous horrors. Today I know the name of that eerie gentleman all too well. The world I knew was filled with crossroads, and it even seemed as if I was slowly turning into one myself.

At that time, these intruders and foreign intelligences never demanded anything. They asked for nothing more than my attention and the curiosity of a child.

No pacts were signed and no blood was ever shed. They would occasionally teach me strange sentences and words, weird symbols and most peculiarly, how to ignite a fiery spark within my own body. Through these sinister games, they were preparing me to become the intruder. In some odd place between waking state and sleep, they were preparing me for the Wholly Other.

Every child owns their inner world of thoughts and ideas, but will inevitably be forced away from it, and find themselves standing in the same dull line as the rest. Memories will turn into childhood fantasies; one world will be destroyed and another one constructed on top of its remains.

It is perfectly possible to alter the past. The lessons taught are stored away in some subconscious part of an inner library, and new realities are constructed on the outside of it. This was the case for me as well. I learned the dogmas and the ethos of this world. The crossroads faded and that sheltering veil somehow rebuilt itself. It may have been for the best. It may even have been a way for the teachers of the liminal plane to keep me out of the bedlam.

They would keep guiding me from afar and sometimes in absurdly humorous ways. Humans who knew the secrets of the veils between worlds would enter into my life now and then. I would sometimes awake while murmuring strange words and the light bulbs would explode as I tried to light up my teenage room. Books would turn up as reminders to revive the faint memories of another reality. In a sequence of events that would fall into the category of coincidence to most, the teachers and mentors eventually returned. They were, however, now of flesh and blood. Without much of a choice, I entered into the esoteric flow of traditions that have survived as an undercurrent in the passing waters of time. Every step down the stairway of life was successively altered by pouring the poison of Samael into the chalice of the past in an intended reversal of our false notion of a continuum. The womb of darkness was impregnated with the semen of forbidden love. This required more than a child could possibly have managed; hence my suspicion that it was planned and designed by some otherness of being. The egg hatched and that other child finally took his first step on the Other side, born from the intercourse of Lucifer and Lilith and delivered by an even older God.

Now, thirty years after the initial meeting at the crossroads, the whole timeline of events is played back in slow motion as I am about to open the doors again. The resounding mantra is the burning key. I can hear that old stranger in the mirror chant and chant until every inch of my existence is filled with the firm determination of fire. The sentence reproduces itself and echoes on the other side of the threshold.

> Zazas, Zazas, Nasatanada Zasas!
> Zazas, Zazas, Nasatanada Zasas!
> Zazas, Zazas, Nasatanada Zasas!

In the distance, the vibrations tears holes in the space time continuum. The lake in-between is birdless and Hermes Chthonios opens the bridge. The waters are divided and the spear is the axis mundi upon which all of existence now depends. In the silence therein, the door stands ajar; a nexus of contending realities and possibilities. Both close and distant in the uttered words. Predicted in every hostile image, in every dismantled dream. Your world and mine will now forever drift apart. Neither silver nor gold will cover its price, for no less than a soul will satiate the night. A knock on the glass and Beli'El becomes my name. Beyond the expanding dullness, in worlds where the surreal is but routine, a raison d'étre is offered by the long-lost Fiend.

THE EXPLORERS
(List of Contributors)

Ingvild Clark (Cover Artist):
"I create art inspired by the occult and mythology, fictional and other, common topics are cosmic dread and the Unknown. Both my interest in the occult and art are lifelong ones. Aside from this, I live in rural Norway and spend a lot of time outside in nature, summer as winter"

Don Webb *teaches creative writing for UCLA. He was the High Priest of the Temple of Set from 1992-2002 and is the author of a few books on Left Hand Path magic including _Uncle Setnakt's Essential Guide to the Left Hand Path._ He has written mystery novels, science fiction, horror and weird fiction. He is a student of Dr. Stephen E. Flowers and lives in Austin, Texas USA with his wife Guiniviere. He likes cats.*

Judith Page *was born in Sydney, Australia. She is an occultist, author, artist, and Priestess of Set. Judith left Australia and studied at Chelsea College of Art, London. Her aim was to study fine art painting but her portfolio demonstrated another gift, and she majored in Stained Glass. She is a recognised member of the Worshipful Company of Glaziers England. Having left art college she went straight back to her first choice, painting, and is an acclaimed artist specializing in the Egyptian Pantheon group. She is also known for her accomplished renditions of the Green Man. Her paintings are in personal temples and private collections, book illustrations and magazine covers for Prediction, Mandrake Books, The Occult Observer, Pentacle Magazine, Neptune Press, to mention but a few. At times she would have to keep her projects secret as many of the paintings would be sold before the paint dried. Her Kabbalah series was seen by the late Kenneth Grant who was so impressed, he asked permission to use the 'Yesod' image first in the black and white publication of The Ninth Arch 2002.*

Jens Frønæs has studied Magic and Esotericism since 1998 and is editor-in-chief at Academia Draconis. He is collaborating with Thomas Karlsson on the autobiographical book series known as the Mephistophelian trilogy which he also translates into English. He works in a clinique treating drug dependency and enjoys books, music and long walks in his spare time. He writes short stories, essays and poetry. He lives in Stavanger, Norway with his wife.

Leo Holmes is a practising magician and an occult enthusiast for more than twenty years, predominantly interested in Chaos Magic, Gnosticism, Thelema and the Typhonian and Draconian Currents. He is an invited member of the Esoteric Order of Dagon - USA, and one of the founding members of the official Brazilian Lodge of the German Ordo Saturni. He has also collaborated with Anton Channing's Kia Invisible Agents and Aeon Sophia Press' The Thirteenth Path Journal. Holmes has written a few occult articles, both in English and in Portuguese, but is better known for his book LeMulgeton: Goetia and the Stellar Tradition, released in 2013 by Fall of Man; and for having collaborated in the translation of The Book of Lies into Portuguese, released by the Brazilian Publisher Daemon Editora in 2018. More recently, in 2019, Holmes published The Abyss, an analysis of the Dark Night of the Soul from an eclectic perspective predominantly inspired by Thelemic Literature.

Paul F. Newman is a professional astrologer whose articles, reviews, artwork and cartoons have appeared in the world's leading astrology magazines. Luna: The Astrological Moon is the companion volume to his first book, Declination: The Steps of the Sun. He is also a freelance copy writer and editor of fiction and non-fiction work for dozens of authors. He teaches astrology at all levels and enjoys the challenge of simplifying and communicating the beauty and complexity of this ancient art to an ever-growing number of seekers.

Suzanne Divinsky began her career as a technician and later switched to quantum physics. From this grew a burning interest in energies and symbols, which in the long run led to the exploration of man's hidden history. The great passion for ancient cul-

tures started in earnest in 2006 after a trip to Turkey.
She is the author of The Wisdom Code trilogy.

Thomas Karlsson (b. 1972) is a world leading LHP practitioner and founder of the international orders Dragon Rouge and Ordo Draconis et Atri Adamantis. He has written nine books translated into ten languages. He holds a Ph.D. at Stockholm University, Sweden, in the history of religion; has three Master's degrees, and is trained in Developing Leadership at the Swedish military's Defense Academy. He is a Fellow Researcher at Yale University, USA and has worked on international educational projects between countries such as China, Brazil and Sweden. Several of his books are bestsellers in contemporary esotericism. He has written lyrics and developed concepts for several metal bands such as Therion, Shadowseeds, Ofermod and Serpent Noir. He has also been involved in producing Techno and Dark Ambient. In his spare time, he devotes himself to his family and to martial arts.

Julien Bert has been studying the Occult and the sacred sciences for a number of years and is the translator of "Qabale, Qliphoth et Magie Goétique" – the French edition of Thomas Karlsson's monumental and most famous work on the dark mysteries which was published in early 2017.
He also contributes regularly to the underground music, art and esoteric journal Zazen Sounds from Greece.
He lives near Lyon, France.

Victor Hernandez is a medical doctor dedicated to allopathic medicine but who also study Traditional Chinese Medicine. "I observe that health and life is not only body or matter, there is something beyond that is in our own psyche and in the cosmos, I combine my academic training with an interest in the occult dedicating myself to the study of hidden themes" He writes poetry and crime fiction short stories.
He lives in Mexico

Jason Schram/ Isfet
"I have been creating music under the name of Isfet for about 11-12

years now in parallel with my magical work, and have been a member of Dragon Rouge for 2.5 years. Aurally, the song is meant to serve as a focus point for entering into the subtle dimensions. The poem, written in a similar style to how Lovecraft wrote his poetry, describes some of the concepts that served as inspiration for the song."

Johannes K: Johannes Kvarnbrink is a Swedish musician, occultist and composer.

─────────────────

[1] From «The Quintessence of Elements» on "Underjordisk Tusmørke" by Tusmørke. Termo Records 2012

ACKNOWLEDGEMENTS

The Editor would like to thank all our contributors for amazing work and patience, the DR books and publications team for suggestions and encouragements, Jason Schram for proof reading, Toby Chappell and Gottfried Fjeldså for the art concessions and Bjørn Frafjord for all the technical assistance.

COMING SOON FROM
ACADEMIA DRACONIS:

Thomas Karlson PhD

Amongst Mystics & Magicians
in Stockholm
· Revised edition 2024 ·

Printed in Great Britain
by Amazon

21450118R00061